MARKED IN FLAMES

ASPEN PACK
BOOK FIVE

CARRIE ANN RYAN

Marked in Flames

An Aspen Pack Novel

By: Carrie Ann Ryan

© 2022 Carrie Ann Ryan

eBook ISBN: 978-1-63695-194-2

Paperback ISBN: 978-1-63695-322-9

Cover Art by Sweet N Spicy Designs

PRAISE FOR CARRIE ANN RYAN....

"Count on Carrie Ann Ryan for emotional, sexy, character driven stories that capture your heart!" – Carly Phillips, NY Times bestselling author

"Carrie Ann Ryan's romances are my newest addiction! The emotion in her books captures me from the very beginning. The hope and healing hold me close until the end. These love stories will simply sweep you away." ~ NYT Bestselling Author Deveny Perry

"Carrie Ann Ryan writes the perfect balance of sweet and heat ensuring every story feeds the soul." - Audrey Carlan, #1 New York Times Bestselling Author

"Carrie Ann Ryan never fails to draw readers in with passion, raw sensuality, and characters that pop off the page. Any book by Carrie Ann is an absolute treat." – New York Times Bestselling Author J. Kenner

"Carrie Ann Ryan knows how to pull your heart-strings and make your pulse pound! Her wonderful Redwood Pack series will draw you in and keep you reading long into the night. I can't wait to see what comes next with the new generation, the Talons. Keep them coming, Carrie Ann!" –Lara Adrian, New York Times bestselling author of CRAVE THE NIGHT

"With snarky humor, sizzling love scenes, and brilliant, imaginative worldbuilding, The Dante's Circle series reads as if Carrie Ann Ryan peeked at my personal wish list!" – NYT Bestselling Author, Larissa Ione

"Carrie Ann Ryan writes sexy shifters in a world full of passionate happily-ever-afters." – *New York Times* Bestselling Author Vivian Arend

"Carrie Ann's books are sexy with characters you can't help but love from page one. They are heat and heart blended to perfection." *New York Times* Bestselling Author Jayne Rylon

Carrie Ann Ryan's books are wickedly funny and deliciously hot, with plenty of twists to keep you guessing. They'll keep you up all night!" USA Today Bestselling Author Cari Quinn

"Once again, Carrie Ann Ryan knocks the Dante's Circle series out of the park. The queen of hot, sexy, enthralling paranormal romance, Carrie Ann is an author not to miss!" *New York Times* bestselling Author Marie Harte

DEDICATION

For the Belles Besties.
Always stay hydrated.
You'll need to in this book.

MARKED IN FLAMES

My mate rejected me, leaving me broken. I refuse to let that happen again—even if Steele is the one for me.

I hold the power of flame and future in my hands, but I know the world is watching. Waiting for us to fall.

The truth and lies that bind the Aspen Pack together are crumbling and I am to bear witness to its fate.

I know the Enforcer of the Aspens is my mate.

Yet neither of us want what fate decrees.

So, we'll fight side by side and ignore the burning attraction between us.

Only when a traitor rocks the foundation of all we know, we might not have a choice to who we cling to in despair.

The vampires were only the pawns in this war.

The demons are on their way.

And if we're not careful, the Aspen Pack could lose someone that breaks them.

And I could lose my mate.

Again.

PROLOGUE

Malphas

Malphas stepped towards the small townhome at the edge of a pleasant neighborhood. He didn't like this area, didn't like that the magical wards from the witches— who had unfortunately regained some of their power— seemed to scrape at his skin. It shouldn't matter, however. In the end, the witches would understand who held the power. They were so cute, with their little magics. Only the ones who came to him to understand the power of blood and were willing to sacrifice actually deserved the power in their veins.

His Lilith understood that, and she let him use her

however he needed. Through power and bond and flesh and everything in between. Lilith held the power that he gave her. And she understood that, without him, she would have nothing.

Malphas was the one with the true power, and these witches and their little coven would soon understand.

He slid his hand over his chest, ignoring that familiar ache. None of the vampires surrounding him noticed. They were busy doing as instructed, getting ready for this step. They didn't realize the witches had gotten a blow in. That death witch had gone down into a version of purgatory, into his hell, and had taken what was his.

She would die just like the others, but first, it was time to collect his trophy. The little songbird to be locked in a cage and would fight and would scream and would burn.

Yes, first he would take her.

"Darling? Are you ready?"

He turned to Lily and slid his thumb over her lips. Her mouth parted, her eyes going dreamy, her pupils dilating. He forced his thumb into her mouth, pressing down on her tongue and gagging her, forcing her to suck on the digit.

"Such a good girl," he murmured.

He slid his finger out, then leaned down and pressed a kiss to her lips. He liked the touch of flesh, liked the way bodies moved against one another when he was in control.

It was why he liked this human body. And why he would take Lily's, and whoever else bowed before him. Lily was not his only lover, but she was his consort and would help him bring down the Aspens.

The Northwest Packs had taken down his brother, but he wasn't as stupid as Caym. The Packs would bow before him.

But first, they needed a witch.

"Burn it."

The vampires—his children—moved as one. He'd made them from his own blood, his own flesh. They were his progeny, his legacy. And he controlled all of them.

Once the vampires learned how to control their own blood, they had some freedom, and they thought that they were in control of their armies, of their destinies. Little did they know that Malphas could pull the cord that would take them to their fate.

They knew nothing, for Malphas was their future. Their only.

"Will we take out the other buildings attached?" Lily asked, her head tilted as she spotted the flames beginning to rise.

Malphas nodded. "Yes. Take them all out. The humans too. They're not needed."

"You do not want to increase our forces?" his commander asked, and Malphas shook his head.

"We have enough for now. The ones in the end unit are part of the Human Union. They will learn what happens when they don't follow us, what happens when they rise against *us*. And not just the filthy mongrel shifters."

The orders given, his commanders moved off as the fire continued to rage.

Malphas held out his hands and began to chant the power of old, of his people.

For inside was a fire witch, the flames within her beckoning. She would've been the perfect consort, the perfect lover, writhing beneath him with agony and bliss. There was something inside her that called to him, something he didn't quite understand. But he would learn what it was once she was under his command.

The flames began to burn higher, and while she could survive the flames like no other could, her power unique in her own right, she wouldn't be able to fight unconscious.

The vampires moved as one and fighting commenced, punctuated by the sounds of people screaming and glass breaking. Malphas stood and watched; they didn't need his power.

With a final scream, Jade was lost to the power and was only for him.

Lily wrapped her arm around his waist, and he smiled as he petted his consort's head.

"She thinks she's all-powerful, leader of a coven of weak witches. But her magic is nothing against ours."

"No, my lover, my consort. She will be ours to play with." Malphas' lips twitched.

"Yes, darling. Ours to play with."

He wanted her power, craved it.

She was the first step in the wolves' unending. In their undoing.

She was the first step in his becoming.

The immortal plane would be his soon enough, but first, he needed a witch.

CHAPTER
ONE

Steele

I EASILY DUCKED THE FIRST BLOW, THEN SHOOK MY head. The man in front of me had bulked out over the past few months, but he still wasn't back to where he used to be. There was a darkness in his gaze, a thinness to his hips. I could no longer see his ribs as he took deep breaths, so there was that at least.

Being dead for as long as Blake Jamenson had been left one's body in a state of weakness.

I rolled out of the way of Blake's next kick, both of our claws out but not doing any damage.

This was a dominance challenge, but not in the ways

that others might think. I nodded tightly, threw my shoulder into Blake's gut, then kept moving, punch after punch, kick after kick, as Blake got out his aggression and showed the Pack who he was, while I let some of my anger slide through.

But this was also a teaching moment.

I was nearly fifty years older than Blake, but Blake had lived a thousand lifetimes.

Although the irony of that meant I would never actually say that aloud.

When Blake and Tatiana had come back from death, or wherever the hell they had been before Dara, our harvester death witch, had brought them back, they had looked exactly like they had when they were killed on the battlefield when the Talon Pack fought the human government. At that point in time, shifters had only recently been forced into revealing ourselves, and some of the government hadn't liked us. Well, that was probably still the case. They had wanted to exterminate us, and some had succeeded. Others, like the man who had helped kill Blake and Tatiana, had wanted to study us.

They had vivisected our brothers and sisters, had torn our bodies apart in order to find a way to create their own shifter super-soldier. And they had nearly succeeded— one of the test subjects was actually part of the Talon Pack now. But the only way that those super soldiers had survived and not turned into grotesque monsters was because of a mating bond.

The government had lost, and now the people in power were friends of the shifters.

It would likely not always work out like that. We constantly had to prove to the world that we weren't or and strong or would kill people with one swipe of a claw near the jugular.

Humans still feared us, with hate groups rising in popularity and threatening us. There were still bills in the government trying to take us out or claim that we weren't human. But we had power too, so we would always find a way to survive.

Just as Blake had.

Just as I had.

Blake moved, claws outstretched, and I took him by the neck, slamming him to the ground.

Blake was strong, stronger with each passing day as he healed, at least physically.

But I was the Enforcer of the Aspen Pack.

It was my sacred duty, a blessing and gift from the moon goddess, to protect my Pack. I had extra bonds to our Pack, much like the Alpha. He could sense the overall well-being of the Pack and be exactly who each Pack member needed, and I fought against the outside forces. If there was a threat to our Pack, my wolf would know.

Only, we had been under threat for as long as I had been Enforcer.

The demons and vampires surrounded us. They were coming for us, so we needed to be stronger, faster, a tighter unit.

And that is why I pinned Blake to the ground as he struggled against my hold.

The others were watching, as this dominance challenge had been sanctioned, but they had seen the way Blake fought.

They saw the strength in both of us.

Blake lowered his gaze, his wolf not as dominant as mine yet, but he had still drawn blood.

He had already risen through the ranks of the Aspen Pack since he had joined us a few weeks ago, but now he was stronger.

I pressed my claws against Blake's chest, feeling the heartbeat underneath my palm. That was good. A damn good thing.

I had known Blake before the war, but we had never been friends. In fact, I had been hiding within the ranks of the Aspens during that time, our former Alpha having not let us help the Talons in any way.

"Yield," I whispered, my voice a low growl.

Blake looked up at me again, his eyes gold with his wolf, before he nodded. "I yield," he gritted out. I smiled, just a quick flash of teeth. I didn't smile often, at least according to everyone who knew me, so when I stood up and held out my hand, Blake looked at it for a second. For a moment I thought his pride would be too much, that the chip on his shoulder was even larger than my own, but he slid his palm against mine and I quickly pulled him to his feet.

The spectators cheered before some went back to their day. Others came towards us, surrounding us. Blake was new to the Aspen Pack, but we were wolves, and we understood how to comfort.

"Good fight," I said truthfully.

Blake smiled. For an instant, his eyes lit up as if he had no darkness within, but then he blinked it away and looked at the others. "I guess nobody can beat the Enforcer of the damn Aspen Pack," he said dryly.

Hayes, our Omega and a six-foot-six tall and broad man who could turn into a polar bear let out a gruff laugh. "You're the idiot who decided to fight against him rather than another dominant right in front of you. But I'd say all of our wolves understand where you rank now."

"I don't know. My wolf just wanted to try it."

"Yeah? Then you did pretty good," Hayes said before he walked off, rubbing his chest.

As the Omega, Hayes could feel every emotion within the Pack. He usually blocked it off, just like sometimes I had to block off my own bonds, but something was rattling the old bear, and he wouldn't tell me. Hayes was on his own most days, if he wasn't hanging out with Wren, our Healer, or Wynter, a human who had been forced to live with us when the human she worked with had threatened her and taken everything from her.

Our Pack was growing by leaps and bounds, just like a healthy Pack should.

The crowd dispersed until it was just me, Blake, and Chase, our Alpha.

Blake immediately lowered his gaze from the both of us, and I did the same to Chase. I might be dominant as hell, but I was nothing compared to my Alpha, or our Beta. Audrey was off with Gavin, the two of them finally taking a moment to themselves.

They had been mated for a few years, for the second time, but with the war with the vampires and demons, they hadn't had many moments to themselves. They were still on den grounds, I could feel them, though I blocked that connection quickly, but they hadn't been here for the dominance fight.

"You're doing well, Blake. Are you aiming to be one of our lieutenants?"

Blake shrugged. "Maybe. I want to thank you again for letting me join. I know it probably isn't easy dealing with me."

I met Chase's gaze for an instant before Chase cleared his throat. "My wife is your cousin, and your other cousin is mated to my best friend. I'm pretty sure we are all turning into one Pack as it is. But I also understand wanting to branch out. You have a lot of siblings and cousins over there."

"And Mom and Dad weren't happy when I decided to leave the Pack, if only for a time."

The Redwood Pack had grieved when they lost one of their own, but now he was back, though he clearly wasn't the same man as before. He wasn't the baby of the family, wasn't all smiles and curly hair. He was different, and though I knew the Redwoods were stronger and tied more emotionally than any other Pack I knew, it must have been a blow to them to realize Blake had changed so much. They gave him space, but Blake needed a change, and both Alphas agreed.

The fact that both Lexi and North of the Redwood Pack were visiting here more often made me smile.

He was still Pack, even if he answered to a different Alpha and not his uncle anymore. There were reasons why a wolf needed space, and the fact our Northwest Pack alliance was strong enough and tightly bound enough to allow that to happen meant we had grown far stronger than others thought possible.

I just wasn't sure we were strong enough to fight against pure evil.

"Are you off to go do some scouting?" Chase asked as Blake walked off with Skye—his cousin and Chase's mate.

"I was thinking about it. How's the baby doing?" I asked, and Chase winced. "Skye refuses to take any time for herself. Doesn't matter that she is about to give birth to our first child, she wants to do everything that she used to do."

"She's a wolf. She can handle anything."

"You keep saying that, but you will rue the day when you realize that your pregnant mate has no concern for herself and keeps putting everybody else first and refuses to just lie down when you ask."

I tried to hide my smile, ignoring the ache in my chest. "Well, that's not going to happen anytime soon, as I have no mate and don't plan on it."

"You're cute thinking you're going to have a choice."

I flipped him off. "And Skye is heavily guarded at all times. I noticed the way that Blake is watching her every move. He's protecting his cousin, just like everyone else. I also see Novah and Cassius walking towards them. What are they doing, ensuring that the precious Alpha's mate doesn't fall and trip?"

"I might have persuaded Novah to walk towards them and ensure that she's safe."

My lips twitched. "Cassius and Novah still trying?" I asked. We began walking towards the perimeter because I needed to do a patrol soon. Chase looked over his shoulder one last time before putting his attention back on me.

"So far. I know that the Healer's working with them, I just hate to see it. Novah wants a child, and Cassius would do anything for her. But you know wolves—we're fertile as hell, unless we're not. There's no middle ground."

I nodded. The Redwoods seemed to have three or more children per family, sometimes up to six. The Talons were slowly following along, as well as the Centrals. We Aspens were taking our sweet time, but then again, we had been scorned by the moon goddess for our past transgressions, much like the Talons and Centrals had. They had overcome it, and we were too. Our Alpha was about to be a father. Adalyn, our former soldier and now Alpha to the Central Pack, was a mother as well.

Our families were changing, our Pack was growing stronger.

"Is anyone placing bets on when Gavin and Audrey start?"

Chase laughed. "Audrey told me that they're waiting until my child's a bit older. They thought that two pregnancies at the top of the leadership might be a bit much."

That made me throw my head back and laugh. "Trust Audrey to try to keep everything on a timeline."

"Hence why the betting pools are increasing. Dara and Cruz are waiting," Chase said, speaking of the Heir of the Pack and our harvester death witch.

"Really? So, it's going to be a while before you are an uncle then?"

Chase grinned. "I hate our father, hate him with every ounce of me, but damn it, I got a brother out of the deal. Took me too long to realize it, but it's pretty damn great."

I smiled as we walked. "Yeah. Our Pack's changing, but we're growing stronger. Hell, we're even working side-by-side with a coven."

Chase raised a brow. I didn't blame him. I didn't usually bring up the witches. Not that I was prejudiced against magic—the exact opposite. No, it was more the fact that one of their coven leaders grated on me beyond all reason.

I did not want to think about Jade though, or her little human friend that was always around. Things got weird when I thought about them. And I didn't want to go there.

"I need to head back, things to do."

"Mate to watch?" I teased.

"My mate is about to whelp a pup, let me be the growly Alpha father here."

"Please use the phrase 'whelp a pup' in front of her. I

want to be there when she rips off your balls," I said with a laugh.

He pushed at my shoulder, my wolf yipping in happiness, before he walked off.

One of my lieutenants came forward soon after, tablet in hand. "Were you just lurking around?" I asked, and Hazel beamed.

"Maybe. Seriously though," she continued. "He's all growly and about to be a dad. I'm going to let you deal with him."

"You're a dominant wolf, you can handle him, Hazel."

"You say that, but then he gets overprotective and forgets that I'm a strong dominant too."

She was all of five-feet, pure strength, and could take down a grown man with her pinky. There was a reason she was one of my top lieutenants, and a good friend.

"I have the latest control reports, as well as information from the Centrals about a potential new kiss."

I sighed and took the tablet.

Demons made vampires. That much we knew. When a demon had slid through the crack from their dark realm nearly thirty years ago, it had created a new being. Blood-thirsty monsters who were either controlled by other vampires or the demon itself. When they gained their own control, and weren't red-hazed and flailing weapons, they were conniving, brilliant, and far more dangerous than any other foe we had ever faced.

When vampires hid together, the groups were called kisses. We would have to find them before they found us. My wolf wanted to stop this. This endless fighting wasn't good for our Pack, and our Healer had said time and time again we needed to find a way to make friends with the vampires, to find the good ones.

Only the man in me wasn't quite sure I believed they were a thing.

"Thanks for the report, are you off shift?"

Hazel nodded. "I have a date," she teased.

"What's her name?"

"Sandy. A cute human with blond curls. She is going to be fun."

"Well, that makes me happy. It's about damn time."

"I leave the den, do you?"

"I left the den last week."

"To what, fight a vampire?"

"Maybe."

"You should go out to the town, to the city. We're not locked in. You're allowed to go out and find a willing wolf or human or witch to tumble."

"Are you telling me I need to get laid?"

"All of our wolves need touch, they need that sensory action. And you, my Enforcer, need to get laid."

She winked, then moved off.

I sighed and thought about the one person my wolf seemed to want these days.

It wasn't going to happen, we had both said as much, but damn it, that witch just wouldn't leave me alone.

My wolf pushed at me suddenly, clawing at my chest as the bonds that connected me to the wards as Enforcer pulsed.

I whirled, moving towards the Pack line before any of my lieutenants or other Pack members noticed.

Then the siren went off, a sentry having noted what I had already felt.

I slammed through the wards, the familiar magic tearing at me. It was welcoming, yet harsh and brutal. Because it knew what was coming, and it knew it needed to be strong.

The wards were filled with the blood and magic of shifter and witch and human. That was what protected us, and I was what protected it.

A single vampire slid out of the shadows, a smile on his face.

"The Enforcer. It's good to see you."

This was a sentient one, strong enough and old enough to fight against any control from its master. I didn't know what set it off, what could change it to be this being. Part of me wanted to see if there were those so-called good vampires out there. Ones that protected. Sawyer told me they existed, but I wasn't sure if I believed Jade's friend.

I wanted to, but the idea of that wasn't quite real.

"What do you want?" I asked as I felt the other members of my team moving around in silence. They were hidden, though I was sure with the vampire's heightened senses he knew they were there. It didn't matter that they were downwind, we all were filled with blood, the vampire's nutrients. He would be able to see us, feel us.

"I'm just here as a warning. I mean no harm." The vampire held up his hands and I growled.

"The demon is coming. Malphas, our master, wants you. Wants your entire Pack. He wants the witches and their power. And he wants the brat about to be born. I would be on the lookout. Because this is only the beginning, he is only the beginning."

At that threat, I threw my head back and howled. The vampire grinned.

We moved at the same time, claws out, but the vampire slid into the darkness, running back to where he came from.

I gestured towards my lieutenants as I ran, but a voice stopped me.

"Steele!"

I whirled at Dara, her eyes wide, magic radiating from her in dark, smoky pulses.

"What is it?" I snapped, the hunt still having me on edge.

"It's Jade."

I paused, the others moving in pursuit of the vampire. I wasn't sure they would be able to catch him, as the vampires were faster than us most of the time when it came to running, not fighting.

"What happened?"

"Her entire complex has burned down, they killed the humans, the children," Dara said quietly.

Cruz was behind her, hand on the back of her neck as he steadied her. My wolf howled, raging at the injustice of it all.

"Dara, where's Jade?"

"The humans and vamps have her. And they left a note."

It felt as if the world crashed around me. "Is she dead?"

Dara shook her head. "I don't know."

"If they have her, we'll find her."

It was a promise I made as Enforcer, and as the man that wasn't Jade's.

Because my wolf refused to mourn until I knew for sure.

I had no link to Jade. I wouldn't know if she were truly dead or not. But there was potential.

Jade, the fire witch full of secrets and flame, was my potential mate, a bond that could be blessed by the moon goddess.

And yet, neither of us wanted the bond.

Only now I was afraid that that one choice might have cost Jade her life.

And mine.

CHAPTER
TWO

Jade

WATER DRIPPED ONTO MY FACE, ONE DROP AFTER another. I blinked, annoyed. Had I left the water on? No, that didn't make any sense. Why would the water be dripping on my face if I had?

I frowned, blinking the droplets off my eyelashes as I opened my eyes, wondering if maybe I had had a little too much wine the night before.

Which would be very unlike me because I never got drunk. Letting myself lose control like that? No, that wasn't me.

I slid open my eyes, carefully, because the light burned, and I froze.

Oh. Flashes came back to me, and things started to make sense though I wished it didn't.

The fire, so hot, as it burned my skin. It shouldn't have been able to do that. I was a witch of fire. An elemental witch, though there was nothing purely elemental about me. Hence why I had never joined the original coven. But we had made a new one from the ashes of those who had perished before us, we had come together with the rejects, the ones that didn't conform, and created a coven. I was a fire witch. I could hold flame in my hand and use it as a weapon.

And yet the fire had burned me when it engulfed my home. The screams of my neighbors echoed in my head, and I remembered them calling out for help. I hadn't been strong enough to save them. Nor strong enough to save myself, it seemed.

I tried to sit up fully and groaned at the pull at my arms.

I blinked again, taking in my surroundings.

Someone had chained me in a stone basement.

There were basements in the Pacific Northwest, though they were still a novelty to me. I lived in South Texas for a few years, on the run from my own demons, and there weren't any basements there because of the limestone and clay. But up here there were basements galore, which didn't make sense to me because there were mudslides and rockfalls due to the constant rain.

And if I kept thinking about the weather and this stone basement, I wouldn't have to focus on the fact that I was chained up. That someone had burned my home down, killed the humans and strangers I had been meant to protect, kidnapped me, and chained me up.

There was only one kind of fire that could burn me, and only when I wasn't prepared.

Demon.

A demon, or someone who had siphoned their powers, had come to hurt me.

I let out a breath, trying to calm myself. I was one of the most powerful witches in existence. I could handle this. I could get out of this myself. I didn't need anyone to come rescue me.

I had been doing things on my own for long enough that I didn't need to worry.

I huffed in annoyance with myself.

No, that wasn't quite true. I had friends now, a coven. I had Sawyer, my best friend who had been through hell and back with me.

They would notice I was gone. They would try to

come get me. But as I sucked in a breath, inhaling the magic around me, I knew I had to get myself out.

There was no way I could allow them to be hurt because I'd found myself in this situation. I protected them, not the other way around. I pulled at the chains, trying to break free, but I knew there was something larger at work.

This wasn't just someone trying to take me and my powers.

This had to be a *demon*.

The same demon who had killed so many, who had created a new fucking species to try to take us all out. Who had sent countless souls to their deaths to try to break through the wards and magic of their enemies. The same demon who was consort to the traitor Lily—who had been a friend to the Aspens for so long. She'd broken her word and her bonds and had killed for her twisted sense of life.

This had to be the same demon. I didn't want to think about the possibility of there being more than one.

Because no matter how strong I was, no matter how strong the Packs and the witches around us were, we were no match for a demon.

To take out the previous demon over thirty years ago had required sacrifice, and they hadn't even killed the damn thing. No, the other demons had taken him back, because apparently he had broken one of their laws.

The fact that one of those demons had apparently stayed behind and begun this war only made things worse.

Before my thoughts could spiral any more than they already had, the door creaked open.

Three men walked inside, their boots stomping along the stone floor. They had large guns pointed down, not at me at least, so I counted that as a win. They wore hunting vests that looked military-like, with sunglasses on even in the dingy light.

I let my senses trickle out, the magic within me draining slowly thanks to the demon-powered bonds at my wrist.

Humans.

These were humans that held me.

Not vampires, not the demon who had infused his magic into these metal shackles.

Humans.

I mentally spat the word.

My best friend was a human. I lived among them. I protected and loved humans.

But these in front of me? No, I wasn't going to be their friend, and from the way that one of them glared at me as he lifted his sunglasses, I knew the feeling was mutual.

I stared at the three men as each of them took off their sunglasses, glaring at me as if I were something stuck on the bottom of their shoe. Only I saw the hatred and knew that if I wasn't careful, I was going to end up talking myself right into the end of their bullets.

They feared the magic within my veins, I could scent it on them.

Magic was real, and it wasn't something men said that women with strong opinions used.

No, it was something they feared much more than a woman with an opinion.

"Well, hello, boys," I purred and could have kicked myself. So much for trying to act innocent and not like I had any power, because the demon magic in these shackles took my power from me.

"Shut up, bitch," the man on the right spat, while the man on the left just smirked at me.

The man in the center, however, smiled softly.

It was that smile that worried me. Not the glares, the sneers. Those I expected.

The absolute joy of having someone captive in their basement was what worried me.

"You sure do have a lot of spunk in you for a bitch who is chained with no help. So odd to think that you believe you have any power here," the man in the center said gently, so softly it was hard to hear him. But I heard, I heard the pleasure in his tone, and knew that if I didn't start acting smarter, I wasn't going to find a way out of this.

"Let me guess, HOG?" I asked, thinking of the Humans Only Group.

Their leader had worked with Lily. But from what we had been able to ascertain from the vampires in our last major clash, HOG—the acronym usually put a smile on my face—hadn't realized they were working with their own enemy.

HOG was a group of humans who believed that humans needed to be put first. First in life, in choices, and in power.

They were so afraid of the power that witches and shifters and vampires and demons held, that they thought we belonged in cages or needed to be killed.

But the hatred behind HOG's message ensured that nothing good could come from them.

The two flunkies snarled at me, saying words so quickly that it was hard to keep up. That's when I realized I must have a concussion. Whoever had knocked me out had rattled more than my nerves.

Damn it.

"We are the Human Union, HU," the man in the center clarified.

"Brand change. That's pretty good. Your other master

wasn't really thinking too hard when they thought of the name HOG."

"Shut up, bitch," the man on the right snapped.

I lifted my chin, trying to find some sense of bravado.

I couldn't get my hands free, but maybe if I annoyed them enough, they would set me free just so they could move me to another location. And then I would get out.

I needed them to give me the key somehow, so if provoking them was going to do it, that was what I would do.

"We prioritize human power. We don't need to be put first, not like our forebears thought."

Forebears. I rolled my eyes. It had been like six months. But sure, if they wanted to label it with historical context, they were welcome to do that.

"We want to work with those with magic to ensure our rightful place. We are not to be stepped upon. We are not the food for those who believe they are more powerful than us. We are a power unto ourselves."

It sounded right, sounded logical, if not coming from the most illogical man I had ever met.

Or at least one of them.

"So you chained me in a basement and killed how many people to get me? I feel special."

"Whore," the man on the left snarled.

I rolled my eyes. "So imaginative. You found me alone in my house, so I must be a whore."

"You're a magic user, you sacrifice others to keep yourself in power."

"That wouldn't make me a whore, not that sleeping with as many people as I wanted would make me one, either. However, that's not how magic works."

At least that's not how light magic should work. I was not a dark magic user. I did not sacrifice animals and humans and my own soul to use power. I had my own. My own that I didn't use to its full capacity because I knew what could happen if I did.

"We're not here to kill you," the man in the center added, ignoring his compatriots.

"Oh? What are you going to do? Ask me out on a date? I thought I was a whore."

The slap came quickly, so quickly I hadn't even had a chance to brace for it. It wasn't one of the two flunkies, it was the man in the center. The man who was so good at controlling his rage.

He hit me quickly, twice on the face, and then kicked me in the chest.

I sucked in gasps of air, trying to breathe.

I glared at him, tasting blood on my tongue.

"Do you feel better?"

"You should hold your tongue before I cut it out," he snarled.

"Well, that would stop me from doing whatever it is you want me to do."

I held back the revulsion of that, because I had meant talking, but from the wicked gleam in the men's eyes behind him, I had a feeling they felt something far more invasive, far more personal.

No, they didn't want me for that. I wouldn't let them. I would die first. And the man in the center knew it.

"We need you as our mole."

I blinked at him. "Excuse me?"

"We need you to tell us exactly what the Aspens are doing. As well as the coven."

I blinked at him, then started laughing as a thin trickle of blood slid from my mouth. "And why am I supposed to do that for you?"

"Because if you don't, we'll kill everyone that you love. Slowly but surely, but first, we'll start with your hope. Your dreams. We'll take those."

I narrowed my gaze at him. "You already have me in a basement, chained with magic. Yes, I noticed that," I said, at the widening of his gaze. "Your group used to be all anti-magic, but I guess once you realized that maybe you do need our power, change was in order."

I expected the slap again, and when he punched me in the ribs, I took it, ignoring the snap.

I just had to hope a shard of bone wouldn't enter my lung, because drowning in my own fluid because I had a smart mouth would suck.

I sucked in air and tried not to move.

He grinned at me, and I pressed my lips together, holding in the scream of pain.

"We know you're special, that magic within you. And master wants it."

I froze because someone had told them. Someone had known or guessed. And I knew who the master was. I knew what he wanted. And it wasn't a mole. It was me.

The men moved in front of me, one taking out a long stick with an electric prod at the end.

My eyes widened, and I tried to press back into the wall. I could be strong. I could fight back, but not when I was chained like this.

When they stuck the cattle prod-like instrument against my body, I screamed, my magic lashing out, wanting to help me, wanting to do anything, but I was chained.

They hit me again and again, and when I finally passed out from the pain, the thought that this could be the end brought with it a sense of peace.

If I wasn't careful, this *would* be the end.

I wasn't out for long, though, and I slowly blinked up at a new person in front of me.

Lily smiled at me, looking angelic and innocent.

But there was nothing innocent about her.

I tasted the magic in the air and knew she was our siphon. The one who had taken the magic from the dead coven. Her demon consort must have taught her that.

Lily wanted power. And she had taken it.

"Well, you seem to have risen through the ranks," I purred, only it sounded more like a mumble.

Lily beamed at me. "Your coven will be dead soon. Your Packs will quickly follow. I can't wait to see them screaming your name when they realize that you could have helped them."

"And how am I supposed to help them? You want me to spy on them for you, that doesn't really make sense, does it?"

"Oh, you see it will. Because if you help us now, if you join us, we won't need you to spy, we won't need you to kill. My beautiful man will help you. Just like you will help us."

I stared at her, uncomprehending.

"You want me to join your side with my magic, for what? To kill everyone who's ever helped us?"

"Not *us*. I was just a sad little partial witch to them. They never saw me. But *he* did."

"He's using you."

"No, but he'll use you. Unless you listen to us, he'll use you."

She crouched in front of me, grinning, as the door behind her opened.

A beautiful man stood in the doorway, with sharp cheekbones and long dark hair. He was possibly the most beautiful man I'd ever seen in my life.

But his soul glared at me, and I knew he was death. My death.

He held out his hand, and the demon magic that I feared, the demon magic that had always called to me, wrapped around my heart and dug in with its claws.

Lily grinned as she shocked me with the cattle prod again while the demon used his magic.

They wanted me to be on their side, so they would break me.

I screamed, not holding back, and knew that I had made a mistake.

They wouldn't be able to find me.

There was only one way to find me within a demon's wards, and that was with a mating bond.

And I had said no.

Now he would never find me.

But I wouldn't break. I wouldn't let them use me.

I would die first, and as I screamed again, pain lashing

at me, I figured death would come a little quicker than I had thought.

But at least I wouldn't betray them.

At least I wouldn't become Lily.

That was the only hope I could hold on to as darkness finally came, and I let it.

And I stopped fighting.

Steele

My bones broke, tendons bending in a new way, muscles sliding together. The fur receded over my skin in a shower of sparks and flame and pain, and I found myself human again. I shook off the dull ache between my shoulder blades and the sensitive skin that came from shifting from wolf to human.

I had done it countless times in my decades of life. And as one of the more dominant wolves of the Pack, and an Enforcer, I could shift back and forth more frequently in a day than others. So when we needed one of us to shift into wolf form and back quickly, it was usually me.

I needed to find Jade, because though she might not be a Pack member, she was still part of us. And nobody was allowed to harm her.

That was the only reason.

"Did you catch that same scent?" Gavin asked, and I nodded at our Tracker.

Gavin was the Tracker of the Aspen Pack because he had been born with extrasensory abilities to track anyone he needed to, as long as he had their scent or they were part of the Pack.

Dara had given us one of Jade's sweaters, and we had used it to begin trailing her scent.

Gavin would find her, and Sawyer and I would ensure that we got her back.

I hadn't been sure I wanted the human with us. It wasn't that I thought that humans were useless or couldn't track, but I didn't know this one. I didn't understand his connection to Jade or why the two seemed to be such close friends. I figured they must have dated previously and had found a way to be normal, but it didn't make any sense to me. Nor was it any of my business. I didn't know what type of skills or powers Sawyer had, other than he had fought alongside us on the battlefield. He had been hurt, bloodied, but never stopped.

He protected those weaker than him from the

vampires and the members of the Human Only Group, so I would trust him some.

Just not totally, as I didn't know him well enough yet.

"I found her," I said as I shoved my feet into the pants Sawyer handed over to me.

"She's gone north, but I think you can tell what else is in that direction," I said, my voice low.

I wished we could talk mind to mind like some wolves could. But those were special bonds, mostly mates. And even if we had been able to do that across Pack bonds, we would be leaving Sawyer out of the conversation, and while I was an asshole, I wasn't a jerk.

"There's a vampire kiss near here. We can usually scent their blood, but they must be using their magic to hide."

Sawyer's eyes narrowed and he nodded tightly. "You scented vampires and humans near Jade's place. That means she could be there, right?"

I rubbed the back of my neck and looked up at Gavin.

Gavin shook his head. "The trail is old, so she was here, but not in the last few hours. At least from what I can tell. We won't know until we go in, and we're going in."

Gavin's jaw tightened, and I nodded.

"We're not letting them keep her. We're going to

figure out what the fuck they're doing and why they want her."

Something flashed over Sawyer's gaze as if he were hiding something, and I snarled.

"What do you know?"

Sawyer lifted his chin. "It's not my place to say anything. I'm just going to find my best friend."

"You'd do better by telling us what the fuck you're hiding," Gavin added.

"I don't know anything." He held up his hands. "I don't know why they want her, but she's a powerful witch, and now that they don't have their coven anymore and are only using that Lily person, they might need her powers."

I snarled again. "Lily and her siphoning. Oh yeah, *fuck*."

"Yeah. Just tell me what to do, and I'll do it. I know you two are the fighters, but I can fight as well." He slid two blades out of his shirt, and I nodded, a smile crossing my face.

"You're damn good with those."

"My best friend can throw fireballs at a group of vampires and not blink. The rest of you can use claws and fangs. It's just the humans in your Pack and me trying to keep up. I'm learning."

"Better with a blade than I am," Gavin said with a shrug before we continued through the forest.

I didn't know how much time Jade had left. I couldn't feel her because she wasn't Pack, which was an oversight on our part. Kind of. She hadn't wanted to join, and I understood why.

Because there was a traitor in our Pack, one that I hadn't been able to scent out, in addition to Lily. She had been two-faced and hid who she was well enough we hadn't figured it out.

So now we needed to find the other traitor.

I needed to know who was selling our secrets to the demon and the vampires.

Jade hadn't wanted to blood into the Pack as a coven member when she couldn't trust us.

And while that hurt, like someone cutting into the bonds that connected me to the Pack, I understood it.

We needed someone on the outside, who was close to us but could hopefully scent betrayal.

But I hadn't kept her safe.

She wasn't mine, she wasn't Pack, but she was still one of ours. I should have done better.

We made a plan as we came across the small cabin that scented of vampire but not Jade.

Her scent had gone off in another direction as we approached the cabin, so she had been there but had been moved.

So hopefully we'd be able to find out through them.

Gavin gestured for me to go on one side of the cabin, Sawyer with him around the other.

I was the stronger fighter, so I nodded tightly, and we moved.

Vampires poured out of the cabin, fangs bared, snarls emanating from their lips.

Two vampires came at me, eyes red, uncontrolled.

Well, damn it. These weren't vamps that could control themselves, so that meant I would have to deal with these fuckers before finding one who could answer our questions.

I moved quickly and sliced through the neck of one and then used my claws to gut the other. They fell easily. These vampires were weak and new.

I wanted to believe that some of them could be the good ones, that they weren't going to fight and try to kill us, but that didn't seem to be the case.

We fought on. I only needed one of them alive to talk to us, but none of these were thinking.

Another broke through the window in front of me, and I took it down, claws outstretched, but stopped just short of killing it when I saw its black eyes.

It snarled at me, claws ripping through my arm. I cursed but kept its fangs away from me. I couldn't let it bite me, couldn't let its venom turn me into a hybrid or whatever else they did to make us into monsters.

Vampire bites on shifters did not lead to good things. And while we had been able to stop the progression of some, others hadn't been so fortunate.

"You okay over there?" Gavin asked as he came forward, blood on his hands, Sawyer right behind him.

Sawyer slid his blades into their sheaths and wiped the blood onto his pants.

"You bit?" I asked them both, and they shook their heads.

"We're fine," Sawyer answered and raised his brow at me, then looked down at the vampire I had pinned to the ground.

"I'm fine too. But this one seemed to have been in charge. Did you get the others?"

"All with red eyes. Damn it," Gavin added.

None of us wanted to kill them. These had been humans that had most likely been changed against their will. But they were controlled by this one. "You going to tell us what you're doing out here?" I asked, my hands tightening around the vampire's neck.

He smiled at me as Sawyer came up, his blades back in his hands.

"You're nothing. A weak little puppy that the master will put down."

I rolled my eyes. "We're done with that now. Your

master isn't mine. But I'm going to figure out what the hell you did with her and why you're out here."

"Where is she?" Sawyer asked.

"I don't know who you're talking about."

Sawyer sighed before stabbing a blade into each of the vampire's hands. It pinned him to the ground so he couldn't claw at anyone anymore, and I raised a brow at Gavin.

"Well, that's one way to do it."

The vampire eventually stopped screaming as Sawyer looked on impassively, arms folded over his chest.

"Tell us."

"Yes, listen to him."

"You're going to torture me now?"

My claws gently pressed against his carotid artery. "I could. I'm damn good at it."

Gavin glanced at me for an instant before he focused back on the vampire.

I had been forced to do a lot of things under our old Alpha. My wolf had died a little each day, but I remembered my training.

I wasn't forced to do it anymore, but I would do anything to protect my Pack. And this vampire wasn't innocent. I had seen the dead bodies through the window in the cabin. He had killed children and bled them for his own feast.

No, there was nothing innocent about this one.

"Follow the trail. You'll find her. She'll be one of us. And we'll have her power. Just like the demon and his consort proclaim."

"They have her then?" I asked, thinking of the demon and Lily.

Lily betrayed all of us, pretending she was weak, innocent, and in need of help.

And then she threatened us all.

It was the worst kind of pain.

I would never forgive myself for trusting her. For believing that she could be the good one.

She killed so many when she betrayed us.

And now she had Jade.

"She'll never go back to you. She'll see the true power."

Sawyer sighed as he went into the cabin, his face going gray as he walked past the pile of dead bodies.

I cursed under my breath as the vampire continued to speak. He had to know something useful.

Sawyer came back out, phone in his hand, and shook his head. "Well, there's coordinates here that seemed to go the same direction as that scent you picked up. So, what do you say?"

The vampire lifted his hands through the blades and came at me again, so I snapped his neck and sighed as he fell down at my feet, a bloody mess, nothing but the pain-crazed monster he had become.

"We need to find her. I'm damn tired of the blood."

Sawyer looked at the death around us, then behind him, and shook his head. "Just a fucking waste."

"It is. So be safe because if you get hurt, and I have to turn you into a shifter to save you, Jade is going to kick my ass."

Sawyer blinked before he grinned. "Isn't that against the law?"

Gavin shook his head as we moved towards the scent that, hopefully, led to Jade.

"Not if it's in writing that you want to be part of the Pack, and it's in your directive. So if you're near death, we can turn you."

"The laws keep changing, it's hard to keep up."

I snorted. "Tell that to a man who's eighty years old trying to keep up with shifter and human law."

"And you don't look a day over fifty," Sawyer teased, and I laughed.

I knew he was doing it to cut the tension, because none of us were prepared. We didn't know what we would find. Jade had to be okay. Because if she wasn't? I wasn't sure what we would do.

We moved on, and I cursed under my breath as smoke billowed in front of us.

"I think we found her," I mumbled.

Sawyer moved first, and I caught him by the back of his shirt. "Stop. Let us figure out what's going on, then you can go in."

Sawyer pushed past me, eyes narrowed. "She has to be in there. Can't you tell? The fire is not human made."

I narrowed my gaze, then noticed the purple and green flames.

No. Even mixed with the oranges and reds of normal fire, that wasn't normal.

"Okay. We'll get her. But you need to stop. Breathe. You go in there, guns blazing, you're going to get her killed."

"She could already be dead, and you're standing out here."

"Then we'll deal with it, but you need to stop. Focus."

Sawyer nodded at me, and then we circled the stone cabin now on fire.

"Do you think Jade did it?" Gavin asked, his voice low. Sawyer wouldn't be able to hear. We weren't hiding from him, but still.

"I don't know. I don't like this."

"Do you sense anyone?" Sawyer asked, practically vibrating.

My wolf pushed at me, he wanted to get in there. Needed to.

"I don't sense anyone else, but there're wards here. Can't you feel them?" I asked.

I held up my hand, my palm brushing against something magic, painful, like glass shards.

Gavin's eyes narrowed as he moved forward. "I didn't. And I should, considering I'm a damn Tracker. But her scent and whatever tracking marker she had stopped right at that line."

These weren't normal wards.

"What are they?" Sawyer asked, as part of the roof fell in, causing more flames to burst into the air.

I narrowed my gaze as I looked up, and pointed towards the space a few feet above the burning home.

"See that? The smoke's trapped like it's in a bubble or something. Whatever it is, it's keeping it contained."

"Then she'll suffocate."

"That means you're going to have to get through these fucking wards. But they're not witch made. They're different."

"Demon?" Gavin asked, and I nodded. "Seems like it. Fuck."

"Then we figure it out. We get in there."

I pressed my hands against the wards, ignoring the pain.

"I think if I use my bonds with the Pack, even this far

away, I should be able to gain enough power for you and Sawyer to get inside."

"She has to be in there," Sawyer repeated. He paused for a moment, then sighed. "I can douse some of the flames."

We turned to him, eyes wide.

"You didn't say you were a witch."

"I'm human. But my best friend is a fucking fire witch. I had to learn a few spells that even I could use to douse flames. You never know."

I looked in surprise at Sawyer. "That would've been nice to know."

"I don't know all your secrets, wolf. Just get me through the wards, and I'll stop the flames." He turned to me, eyes wide. "I'll need...I'll need help. And to do that I'll..."

My wolf growled, but I knew what this choice would mean and how Sawyer was willing to change everything to protect his best friend.

After the decision was made, my bonds as Enforcer stretched, and the others shook off the magic.

"I'll help you both get through the wards," Gavin assured us, his eyes gold with his wolf.

Gavin and I pressed our palms against the wards. He let out a hiss of breath, the pain rocking him just as much as it did me.

It was a thousand tiny needles against my skin.

But I could get through. I had to.

I knew just as well as they did that Jade was in there.

They had left her trapped in there to die.

I'd be damned if we let it happen.

I pushed through, ignoring the blood dripping from my ear, the burn marks along my skin.

My wolf tugged at the bonds between Alpha and Enforcer, between Pack and Enforcer, and then we were in, the wards falling at our feet.

I wasn't sure I should have been able to do that. Maybe this was a trap, and the demon had done this on purpose.

It didn't matter in the end because I had to find her.

I had watched people I loved die. I had killed people I hadn't wanted to. I would be damned if I let Jade die if I could help it. She was a witch, and she had too much spunk to die like this.

We moved in tandem as Sawyer chanted, the flames dying back some. They weren't all out, but it was enough for me to get through.

I knew Gavin would keep an eye on Sawyer, but I had to go.

Jade was there. She had to be.

I turned the corner, pushing my way through a wall when I scented her, when I finally saw her.

She was bloody, broken but breathing.

She was curled into a ball on the ground, broken chains around her.

Rage tore at me. They had fucking chained her.

No one should ever have done that. Not to her, not to anyone. But especially not to her.

She was light, fire, and strength.

And they had threatened that.

I threw myself towards her as a log on fire fell from the ceiling. It slammed into my shoulder, but I ignored the pain, and pushed hair from Jade's face.

They had done a number on her, the cuts and burns making her nearly unrecognizable.

But I knew Jade.

I could feel her in my soul, the way that my wolf yearned.

I knew who she was for me, who she couldn't be.

I cupped her face, careful not to move her, and her eyes opened at my touch, making my wolf howl.

"Knew you'd come," she rasped before she coughed, her body shaking.

"Did they hurt your spine?" I asked, not sure what else to do.

"I'm fine. Just a few ribs."

"I'll get you out of here. I promise, Jade. I'll get you out of here."

"And then we'll make her burn. Make both of them burn."

She didn't have to say who *they* were. But then she passed out again. I cradled her to my chest, holding back my own rage.

Because she was so tiny, so broken.

And with every step, I knew if she hadn't been passed out from the pain she would've cried out, and Jade never would've wanted anyone to see her like that. I was thankful for that small mercy.

We would stop this, we would hurt those who had hurt her.

Once she woke up.

Because she had to wake up.

"I've got you, Jade. I've got you."

And if I hadn't known for sure that she was passed out, unconscious, I would've sworn I heard her say "I know."

Of course, that wasn't the case.

But my wolf could dream.

FOUR

Jade

I IGNORED THE PAIN IN MY RIBS AS I SAT UP IN BED, reaching for my book.

"What did the Healer say?" Dara asked, and I glared at my best friend in reply.

Ever since they had brought me back to the den to fix me up, Dara hadn't left my side. The fact that Sawyer wasn't here as well meant that somebody had finally forced him to go sleep. He looked exhausted when I had first opened my eyes, and I knew he hadn't slept at all the entire time I'd been unconscious. He had also been searching for me, and I would be forever grateful for that, and yet I needed my other best friend to sleep.

The fact that he hadn't before now meant he was far more worried about me than I thought. That, and he had used too much of whatever magic humans had in order to try to save me.

I had never thought that the power I had taught him to use, however finite, would have been able to save me and keep the others safe. I had taught Sawyer those few incantations in the event that he needed to get to safety, to run away, to save himself after I had blown everything else up. Because with the power deep inside me, that was always a possibility. Then again, I should have known that Sawyer would never run away. He would never have tried to protect himself when he could protect me.

The man was annoying like that.

Now he was hopefully somewhere sleeping, or the Healer had forced him to pass out. If only my other best friend could give me the courtesy of enough space to breathe.

Dara looked so much lighter than she had in the past. It wasn't the magic within her. No, that hadn't changed. If anything, she had twined closer to death, and she didn't fear it as she once had.

However, while she might feel like she was carrying the weight of the world on her shoulders, she also had her mate to rely on, and a Pack and coven who would be there for her.

I wasn't a Pack member. The people surrounding me still weren't getting that. I had tried to make it clear to them that I didn't require the bonds they had. And if they tried, they would end up hurting everyone else. But they didn't seem to listen.

It was as if me joining the Aspen Pack was a foregone conclusion. Too bad they didn't know what I did, or the reasons for me to stay far away.

"You're glaring," I said, and Dara just rolled her eyes.

"Only to match your glare. Seriously. You almost died. And it's only the magic of the coven that you finally let help you that healed most of your bruises and cuts. You didn't see how you looked when you first came here."

I held back the wince at that. I knew I must have been bad because I could still feel the pain.

I didn't heal as quickly as shifters did, but with the power of the coven, I should have been out of bed and dancing by now. The fact that I wasn't told me that I was far more hurt than I thought.

But I had survived. My friends, the Aspens, had found me.

He had found me.

I tried to ignore the memories of his voice in my head,

telling me I was safe now, that I was in his arms. I didn't want that to comfort me. I didn't want to lean on that.

I knew better. It wasn't going to be forever. It couldn't be forever.

"I'm fine. Truly. I thank all of you for everything you've done, but even though my ribs are still a little sore, I need to get up and move around, and figure out what I'm going to do next."

I was fully clothed, laying under a blanket, as Dara studied my face.

"I want you to be okay, but if you're not okay I need to know that too."

"Don't worry about me. I'm fine."

She raised a brow.

"Okay, I might not look like I'm fine, but I am."

"Your house burned down while you were inside. I'm so sorry you went through all of that."

"It's not your fault. You know that. It's those who want to take over our world. We know how they work, what they want, but we'll figure out how to stop them. You are not to blame for their actions."

"Why does it feel like I'm to blame?"

"You're gaining a complex." I winked as I said it, and she rolled her eyes.

"Seriously. I'm going to get out of this bed now, I need to stretch, okay?"

I moved my legs out from under the blanket and stood up, Dara holding her hands out to catch me if I fell.

I wanted to hate her a little bit, but it wasn't her fault. She was just trying to keep me safe.

However, I was feeling a little hemmed in. And though it wasn't her fault, I was ready for space. And to figure out what the hell that demon and his little bitch wanted from me.

It wouldn't be as easy as them wanting me to pass on information. No, they wanted something else. Something I would never give them. Even though I knew it would mean my death.

"See? I can stand."

"Well, you're staying here," she said, and I raised a brow.

"And you're going to make me?"

"No, but I could," a deep voice said from the doorway, and I turned to see Chase, the Alpha of the Aspen Pack standing there, fists at his side, eyes narrowed.

His wolf was in his gaze, but I had a feeling it had nothing to do with me. No, his mate was due any day now. Therefore, he was a wolf on edge, ready to gut anyone that came close to his family.

I didn't blame him. There was a world out there trying to kill the wolves and anything magic. And a pregnant Skye with all of her glowing radiance and light was a beacon to those who hated what was different.

"You're Alpha, this is your land, but I'm not Pack. You can't tell me where to stay. I appreciate all that you have done for me, though."

He snorted, and I raised both arms, careful of my soreness. "I do. You saved me. All of you did, and I will be forever grateful, however, I need to keep close to the coven."

"I do from here," Dara pointed out, and I sighed.

"You do. And I love you for it. But not all of us can live within the den and join the Pack. We need that independence. I need that independence."

Chase stared at me and I lowered my gaze. I might be a dominant, as the wolves put it, but I was nowhere near Chase's level. There was something different about him and the Alphas. Even a witch with an authority problem knew that much.

"I need to go back to the coven and figure out where I will live."

"You can live here."

I stared at Chase, and I knew he wasn't being obstinate on purpose. He needed me to be safe because I was friends with his Pack, and this was the way for him to ensure it.

I didn't know if he knew what I did. I needed to tell

him, but I wanted to come with answers. I didn't want to raise more questions without a solid plan. But if I wasn't careful, I was going to run out of time.

"Can we leave this small medical room and have you both stop staring at me and telling me what to do?" I asked, trying not to sound like a petulant child, but everyone was taller than me, so I didn't think I was successful.

"Can we at least have this conversation outside of this small medical room? You're towering over me, and I don't appreciate it."

Chase raised a brow while Dara just rolled her eyes.

Nearly all of the wolves were far taller than me, with that polar bear being the tallest of them all. They all could break me with one pinky, and yet my power was stronger than theirs. At least in some aspects. Only, they couldn't tell that when I was cowering on a hospital bed.

And that's how I felt.

Cowering because I wasn't strong enough to take care of myself. Because I had lost. I didn't want to lose again.

I didn't want to be beholden to them either. Not when I knew something was coming. Or perhaps it already had.

The Alpha nodded and took a step back, gesturing for us to follow him.

Dara narrowed her eyes at me before she left, and I knew this wasn't the last of it.

Dara had always been this way, throwing herself into trouble to protect everyone else. And those in her circle, she wanted to be close if needed, safe.

And I suppose I was one of them now.

As were the other members of the newly made coven.

I followed them and then cursed when I realized there was a reason the Alpha had capitulated so quickly.

Now I was far outnumbered. Not in just in personality, but power and everything else.

"Is this an intervention?" I asked, my voice deeper with held-back annoyance.

The Healer shook her head, leaning against the doorway. She was the only person smaller than me in this room, tightly compact, a lynx in a human body. She held a quiet power, one that I wasn't sure everyone else could see. Or perhaps I was wrong. After all, they were all connected on a spiritual and soul level. Perhaps they knew exactly what power stood in this room.

"You're staying with us. You don't have a choice."

I straightened my shoulders as Dara's mate sighed and put his hand on her shoulder. "I'm not sure that was the right way to start," he mumbled.

Everyone else was able to hear exactly what he said. After all, they were all shifters, and their senses were keen.

"I'm not staying with you, Dara. You're newly mated and need space."

Sawyer came in through the hallway and I sighed. "You're supposed to be sleeping."

"I could say that about you. Stay here, Jade. Within the den. I have been, and I'm staying right here in the thick of it. There's no other choice for me and we both know it."

I took a step back, shock hitting me. This had always been a pausing point for us. At least I had thought so. A place where he would fight alongside me but be *safe*. Not his home. "Are you serious?"

"Yes. I had to."

"What do you mean by *had*?" I asked, flames tickling at my fingertips.

Dara cursed under her breath as the Alpha just raised a brow.

"The human needed more power," Chase said, and I whirled on Sawyer.

"No, you didn't."

"To save you I did. I blooded in. I had already been thinking about it. I needed to do something. I can't just stand by helplessly and wait for you all to save me. So, I blooded into the Pack. I don't know what happens next, and we don't have to make a decision now, but I'm staying here. This is where we're meant to be. Don't you see that? Don't you understand that?"

I stared at him, uncomprehending. Sawyer had always been the loner. The fact that he had even stayed with me as long as he had was a testament to our friendship.

The idea that he had blooded into the Pack, had bound himself with bonds that were not easily broken, shocked me.

He was theirs now. Connected to the damaged shadow that I wasn't sure they realized existed.

I looked up at another set of eyes in the room, and knew that perhaps they did know, because Steele had to know.

"Okay. It seems I'm outnumbered."

"Fuck it," Steele growled, and I whirled on him.

"What? I just agreed."

"There's a spare cabin. You don't need to stay with Dara, but you should stay on the den grounds. I can't keep Dara's friends safe while Lily has a hard-on for you, so get over it."

The room was so silent I could hear the slight gasps from the others.

I met Steele's gaze, because I could, I always had been able to.

"I will not be Pack."

Wren, the Healer, sucked in a breath. I looked at the

Alpha, then my best friends, and then back at Steele. "I cannot be connected to a Pack that has that shadow."

The room was silent, even though I had spoken of this before.

"You have a traitor."

Steele growled but nodded tightly. "We know. I felt it along the bonds."

Relief cascaded into me, even though I knew this wasn't the end.

Chase cleared his throat. "I've caught a glimpse. I thought it was Lily. But we have another traitor. We will find them because I'm damn tired of our Pack rotting from within."

"And that means someone is hiding that traitor from you with magic. That's the only way they would be able to last this long. I know the health that comes from the hierarchy of this Pack. You are all strong and want to do good. You have your own issues, but I probably have more issues than all of you," I said with a hollow laugh. "So I suppose I will help. But I cannot be Pack. I cannot bond with you."

At that, I turned and left the building, doing my best to hold my hands still at my side and not shake.

I was so afraid that Dara would follow me, would want answers. But I didn't have answers for them.

Of course, it wasn't her that followed me. It was him.

It was always going to be him.

We turned the corner, and I stood under the tall redwood tree, breathing in the air as I tried to let nature and magic sink into me.

"I cannot stay for long. You know that."

"I do. But you can't be on your own. Not when the danger's out there looking for you."

I didn't look at him, I couldn't. Not when I needed to say the rest. "And when I said bonds, I meant all of them." A pause. "I cannot be your mate."

"Good, because I don't want that either."

I let out a hollow laugh and ignored the hurt. That ache slammed into me, but I ignored it.

"Good."

And then I let him lead me to the cabin, my small box of possessions in his hands. The only things left from my past as I tried to walk into my present.

I would find the traitor, and I would find out what this demon wanted from me.

Then I would walk away.

Before I let a wolf hurt me again.

CHAPTER
FIVE

Malphas

MALPHAS PACED BACK AND FORTH, ANGER COMING IN spurts. Catching that fire witch had been a problem. He knew it would be, but it needed to be done. There was something within her that worried him, and not much worried a demon. After all, he was the power of death itself. How could anything attack him? But the death witch had tried, and she nearly succeeded, not that he would let anyone know that.

But that fire witch, something else was there. Something that he needed. Her magic was special, so much so that he wasn't even sure she understood it.

"Consort?"

Malphas turned at Lily's voice, annoyed at the interruption of his thoughts. She was always doing that, wanting more and more attention, she who had just an inkling of power and wanted more. She craved it, so Malphas had taught her to siphon.

She was now a pure siphon who craved the energy and magic of her hosts. She would demand more, and Malphas would give it to her, because she was just one step.

She was the connection to humanity that his demon craved.

But Jade...Jade was another. Malphas needed her. She would be *his*.

"What?" Malphas snapped, before he noticed the narrowing of her gaze. She didn't like when he yelled, but she did like when he shoved her against the wall. Her eyes flared then, his hand around her neck. "Is there something you wanted, pet?"

Malphas slid his hand between her legs and she moaned. She was wet for him, always wet for him.

"You. Always you."

"Was there something else, or did you just need my cock?"

"Both."

Malphas smiled, took her hard against the wall as she

moaned and clawed at his back. She came quickly, and he followed. It was what she wanted, what they both wanted. At least what Malphas wanted for now.

He was almost done with her. Not that she knew it. She would understand soon.

When Malphas sacrificed her.

But she didn't need to know that yet.

"What's next, my love?" Lily asked as she cleaned them up.

"We test the barriers. The wards will be changing soon, but we both knew that would happen."

Lily beamed. "Our insider. They'll get us into the den?"

"Of course. They'll get us in just like they have before. They're already getting us news of who's coming, which whelp will be born soon. They will get us the babe."

"And *her*...you still want her?" she asked, jealousy dripping through her tone.

"Yes," Malphas said softly, his fingers pinching her chin hard enough to bruise. She parted her lips, before she smiled. "She'll be for us," he lied. "And then the world will be ours."

"Good," she whispered, and as he crushed his mouth to hers, he knew part of him would mourn when he killed Lily.

Malphas had grown fond of his consort.

But he needed Jade and whatever power burned within her.

So maybe Malphas would kill the one she seemed to desire. Or do something worse.

He smiled against Lily's lips as he took her again on the floor. Yes, he would do something worse.

CHAPTER
SIX

Steele

MY WOLF SLEPT BUT WAS STILL ALERT. I WAS ABOUT to start my routine perimeter check, and my wolf would wake, and we would be ready.

I hadn't been able to sleep the night before. Neither one of us had. Not with the conversation with Jade sliding through my mind. I hadn't been able to sense what she felt, what was beneath those words.

I wasn't sure I wanted to know what her true feelings were, beyond the words she said. She was safe within the den wards, and that was about all I could hope for at this point.

It didn't make much sense to me, but then again, nothing did in this war.

I wasn't sure anything was supposed to.

"You must be deep in thought for you to not even growl at me for wanting to walk with you."

I looked down at my Alpha's mate and lifted my lip in a fake snarl.

Skye rolled her eyes.

"You are so fearsome. Oh no, whatever am I supposed to do?"

This time I let out a slight growl, which made her laugh, her hands on her stomach as we walked.

Though I was on my way to my shift, I was still keeping half of my attention on Skye, making sure she didn't trip, and being on alert in case anything happened.

"Okay, now you're watching me like I could take a tumble at any moment. We are walking on flat land, and I'm watching every step. I also know that three of your lieutenants are in hearing range, just in case I were to stub my toe. I'm fine."

I snorted and shook my head. "You are two days past your due date, and Chase had to leave the den to go work with the local government. He is most likely sitting across the table from the governor, trying not to rip the man's head off."

Skye sighed. "He had to go. I forced him to go. And he's in easy driving distance in case he needs to get back."

"You say that, and even though he's one of my best friends, he will murder me if you get hurt. I might be the Enforcer, but he's my Alpha. I know that they wanted the four Alphas there, but I don't like all of them being in one place. Nor do I like not being there."

My wolf was awake now, prowling and stalking. Neither one of us were really happy that we weren't by our Alpha's side.

"Two of the Alphas are there, and Audrey is there so there's a Beta there as well. And they're not all in the same room. They're in two separate places, talking to the mayor and the governor. And you know that they have all of the security that they need."

I heard the slight tremor in her voice, the fear she was trying to hide.

"Are you convincing me or yourself?"

"I would flip you off, but I'm too tired."

Instantly on alert, I looked down at her and noticed the tension in her eyes, the slight pain when she rubbed her lower back.

"You're having contractions, aren't you?" I snarled.

At that, three elders, two maternals, and two lieutenants were at our side. Skye narrowed her wolf-gold eyes at me.

"They just started. I was trying to give everybody time before we called Chase back. He's already probably half out of his mind being separated from me. So please, let's not overreact."

"Okay, Mama," Wren said as she came forward, hands outstretched. The Healer looked ready to bolt, and I didn't blame her. Skye wasn't a dominant, but she was Gamma, and even before she was the mate of the Alpha, she was outside the Pack structure. That meant that she had dominance over all of us.

"I will go back with you to the clinic. And I will rest, mostly because if Steele has a heart attack while he's watching me, Chase won't be happy losing his Enforcer."

As soon as the words were out though, she bent over, hands on her stomach as she grunted.

I scooped her up, holding her close to my chest as I practically ran towards the Healer's clinic, Wren right behind me.

Everybody looked alarmed, but Skye waved them off.

"It's just a contraction. I'm fine."

"I'm calling Chase now," Cruz said, holding out his phone.

"I'm really okay," Skye said, before she shook her head. "But maybe call Chase anyway."

I set Skye on the bed before I was pushed out of the room, Wren blocking the way, along with Hayes. Apparently the Omega would be there for her as well. Other people moved in, but I just stood back, knowing it was best if I wasn't around. However, I was going to do what I was good at—making sure my Pack was safe.

I went back on patrol, and everybody who saw me started asking questions, wanting to know what was going on. I didn't have updates for them, but smiled as a car came barreling down the road, and Chase practically jumped out of it while it was still moving.

Audrey parked, jumped out, and shook her head. Her hair was wild, and she stretched her hands out.

"You okay?" I asked.

She snorted. "Oh. Just fine. Chase was shaking too much to actually drive, and wanted to run here as wolf. I could get us here faster."

Her mate slid out of the back seat, shaking his head. "I've never actually seen a car go that fast. The fact that there was a police escort so we wouldn't get a ticket was quite nice. The governor says congratulations but will keep the news of it contained to the people in the room," Gavin said as he wrapped his arms around his mate. Audrey sighed and looked around the people who were gathering. "I'm going to go check in to see what I can do. You're on patrol?"

"I'm heading towards the outer perimeter. Routine, but with this going on, I want us on a higher alert."

Audrey nodded tightly. "You're the Enforcer. Sounds like a plan." She let out a breath, a smile creeping over her face. "Well then. We're about to have a new Pack member."

I nodded, my wolf perking up, wanting to meet this new Packmate. It would happen soon. Chase would be a father, and the Alpha's child would be protected. My job meant I needed to guard the perimeter.

When I heard a cheer, I turned to see Audrey jumping into Gavin's arms.

"The baby's here! It's a girl!" I smiled, then threw my head back, howling. Others joined in the celebration, a bear roar shaking the ground around us. Dark spirals of magic flew into the air, settling into the wards as protection, and I knew Dara was celebrating with us.

Everybody milled about, happiness abundant, and I knew that the line to see the baby when it was time would take days. But wolves loved children, they were Pack, our tiniest members who needed all of us.

And I would be there as Enforcer, and as an honorary uncle. But I needed to keep the Pack safe and I had a bad feeling. I didn't know if that was because I had a new member to take care of, or if something was coming.

I moved right outside the wards. It was harder to get through the wards right then if something came, and I needed all of my senses. My two partners took flanking positions, and we moved through the forest, jogging as we tried to keep alert.

That's when I noticed the first footprint.

I held up my hand to stop, so we could take a closer look, when the explosion came.

I flew back, slamming into a tree, but landed on my two feet. I shook off the pain, looked at my lieutenants, who both nodded, and then we moved to figure out what the fuck just happened.

I jumped over a fallen tree right as I heard the alarm go off in the den. I barked orders to my team over my transmitter, hoping they could hear through the sound of a roaring fire.

"Truck bomb," my lieutenant said.

"Fuck," I growled as the first vampire came.

It came at me and I lashed out, claws out, fangs bared. This one wasn't one of the ones with control.

It snarled at me, eyes red, someone else controlling it. I would have to figure out who was in charge and get them down. Once you did, the horde was easier to handle.

My claws slid into the vampire's chest as it tried to bite me. I twisted its neck and it fell at my feet with a resounding thud. The next vampire came at the man on my left, but my team had him down, and I went for another and another.

The demon in charge of all this had to be going

through countless soldiers. How long had he been collecting humans and turning them? How many of the missing humans that we were hearing about in the news were in front of us now, dead beyond reason because they didn't have the control to make the choice on their own.

I wasn't sure I wanted to know the answer to that. I wasn't sure I could handle it.

While other vampire skirmishes were happening around the country, and the world, most of it was centered on us, on our alliance.

I didn't want to focus on what would happen next, not when I needed to stop what was happening now.

I saw a flash of red hair in the corner of my eye, and I whirled, seeing Jade standing on the edge of the wards.

From her comfortable attire, it looked as if she had been meditating on the coven grounds, and now she stood between the two sets of wards, flames out.

She barreled through one of the vampires, but her flames didn't seem as bright as usual.

There was something off about them, or maybe I was just seeing things.

I knew she was still tired, had been meditating for a reason. She had almost died, and while I took the vampire down next to me, Jade didn't see the one behind her.

I moved, running faster than I ever had in my life.

"Jade!" I shouted.

She looked at me, then turned as quickly as she could, flames out, but it wasn't fast enough.

The vampire slammed her to the ground and her head thudded against the soil, her flames dissipating.

What the hell was going on? She was one of the strongest fire witches I had ever heard of.

She pushed at the vampire, but it was far stronger. I was there, fast, and with my claws out, I shoved the vampire off her and ripped its heart out in one movement. Blood seeped over my claws, and I looked down at Jade, at the grayness in her eyes, and cursed.

"Are you bit?"

"No. I'm fine."

The truck that had exploded was still on fire, the gas tank about to go, and I threw myself over Jade, covering her with my body.

She pushed at me, shouting obscenities, before I finally rolled off her and looked around at the dead vampires and the fact that there were no more attacking.

"I was fine. I had him."

I lifted a brow. "No, you didn't."

"I'm a fire witch. I can't burn. Thank you for the assist, but I had it."

"You almost died. I saved you. Get over it."

She continued to shout at me, but I ignored her.

I knew she was yelling at me not because she had

needed saving, but because it was me who saved her. My wolf worried about her. Not the man. Never the man.

I looked around at the dead bodies and shook my head as Jade quieted and sighed next to me.

Neither of us said anything, and I wasn't sure there was anything to say.

We had won the battle, but it was a tiny skirmish, just something to test our defenses.

I was sweaty, covered in blood, and exhausted.

"Get back into the wards. I can't protect you out here."

"I don't need your protection, Steele."

"It seems you do," I said, before I went to my lieutenants, leaving her behind, knowing she would go back into the wards. Not because I said to, but because it was the only thing she could do.

By the time I cleaned up everything and gave my reports to Audrey, since Chase was busy with his new pup, I was exhausted and just wanted to get clean and do anything but deal with war.

I was the Enforcer. I should be used to this, but I sure as fuck didn't feel it.

I stripped down in the hallway and made my way to the shower, turning the jets on full, as hot as they could go.

I stepped underneath the stream of water, letting the

boiling temperature practically scald my skin. But it would help soothe the anger.

As soon as steam began to fill the room, I heard the familiar creak of the door opening.

I scented her through the steam, and I didn't care.

My shower was an open stone structure in the bathroom, with no glass walls or curtains, so it wasn't like I could hide anything, and I didn't care to.

I turned and looked at her as the water slammed into my back.

Jade just glared at me, and I was done. So done.

"You know, if you wanted my cock, you just had to ask."

I hadn't meant to say the words, I was just so damn angry.

Jade lifted her chin. "I'm not a damsel, I never have been. So you can just put that cock away."

I grinned, knowing the game was on.

I just wasn't sure if we should play at all.

CHAPTER
SEVEN

Jade

THIS WAS SUCH A MISTAKE. SUCH A STUPID FUCKING mistake. But I couldn't leave. My feet were cemented to the ground, the floor reaching up and holding me still.

There was something wrong with me—I didn't want to leave. I couldn't leave.

Neither of us wanted this, yet that was a lie. We just didn't know what would come after.

He stood there, looking like a damn god, but I didn't know why I wanted him. No, that was another lie. I knew why I wanted him. And I knew why I couldn't have him.

This was the worst time for this need to flare. Neither

of us should fall into each other as if we didn't have the rest of the world waiting on us.

There were more important things going on in our worlds than our needs.

He turned to face me completely, and I couldn't keep my gaze from going down to that cock of his. He was long and hard and thick. And when he turned, it bobbed up and tapped his belly.

He would fill me, and he would make me come. I knew that just from the way he moved when we trained.

The way he rubbed his hands all over me when I tried to fight off the vampires before.

There were reasons I needed to be away from him. But I couldn't think about them in that moment. No, all I could think about was what I wanted. What I craved.

"If your eyes keep drifting down, I'm going to make you go down on your knees and discover what it tastes like."

I met his gaze, flames licking at my fingertips. "Assertive, are you?"

"Always. But you're the one staring at my dick."

"You're the one standing naked in the shower."

"I was here first. I was trying to clean off the blood and muck from that battle. You walked in here. So, are you going to tell me what you want? Or should I just go back to cleaning myself while you watch me?"

He slid his soapy hand down his length, and I held back a groan.

"Steele."

"Yeah?"

"For some reason I have jokes about that steel in your hand, but I suppose you've heard them before."

He paused for a moment before he threw his head back and laughed, water sliding over his skin.

He was beautiful when he laughed, but I wasn't sure I had truly ever seen him do it other than in mockery of his own actions.

But he was beautiful, and strong. He was the Enforcer for a reason, and not just because the moon goddess demanded it.

He was everything. But he wasn't mine.

I knew that, and so did he.

"I don't need you protecting me," I said after a moment, trying to regain my composure.

Steele just tilted his head at me, in that wolf way of his, before he turned back to the water and washed off the soap.

"I'm a dominant wolf. I'm the Enforcer of the fucking Pack. I know my place. My duties. Maybe you should sit down and actually think about yours."

Anger burned, just as the flames at my fingertips did.

"You're an ass."

He snorted and stared at me. "Yeah. I am. But you knew that going in. You've always known I was an asshole. I didn't protect you because I thought you couldn't take care of yourself, I did it because I was in the moment and knew that I could. There was a vampire on you, I wasn't going to stand by and watch it attack you when I was able to stop it."

"I had it."

"We both know you didn't," he said softly, and I wanted to fling flames at him. To do anything other than acknowledge he was right.

"I had it," I whispered.

"Maybe. But I didn't see that. You didn't get hurt, and neither did I."

I looked down at the cuts on his arms, grateful I didn't see any bites. I didn't know what I would do if he got hurt because of me.

"I don't need you to protect me. I need you to get out of my way."

"You're the one watching me shower, firestarter."

That made me snort, and I shook my head. "I'm good with flame, I'm good with magic. I've always been able to fight for myself."

"Like I said, maybe. But I'm not sure why you're in here yelling at me. I protect a lot of people, not just you."

"You're the one that growled at me to stay here."

"You want to find the traitor? Then help."

I wanted to. I needed to. I needed to protect my friends and family. They were all I had left. But there was a yearning between us, a connection we were both ignoring.

I didn't know his reasons, and I didn't want to think about them because if I did, then I would break.

Because if he acknowledged the connection between us, that meant he was rejecting me, and I wouldn't go through that again.

But there was something there. Something we needed to discuss. Even if I hated it.

"I can't be your mate."

He looked at the flames in my hands, then up at my face.

"That's fine."

I laughed, but there was nothing humorous in it. "No. I won't be your mate. I've done this before." I didn't mean to say that, but his eyes narrowed, the shower still going, so I relented. "I fucked a wolf, the moon goddess called. She proposed that we would be mates, that I could be his forever. And then he left. He left and he didn't look back because I wasn't what he wanted. He wanted a wolf, and a witch wasn't going to do. I see the way you look at me, I feel that. But I will not be rejected again. I am not fragile, but I will not be that vulnerable again. So, no matter what happens, no matter what battles we fight, no matter what enemies we face, I will not be yours, nor will I allow you to walk away from me."

I had never told anyone that. I hoped to take that secret to my grave. But I couldn't, and we both knew why, even though I hated myself for it.

He didn't say anything. I needed him to say *something*.

So I turned on my heel.

But then he was there, pressing his wet body against me. I shivered, the magic within me flaring.

"You're going to leave just like that?"

"There's nothing for me here."

He laughed again, and it was so deep that it rumbled right through me. I could feel the hard press of his cock at my back, the wetness of his body sinking into my clothes.

I grew wet too, and I barely resisted the urge to press my thighs together. But he could scent it, and he shivered, pressing his nose to my neck. I closed my eyes and breathed in.

I was powerful, but so was he.

I wasn't sure what I was supposed to say.

"Fucking only—if that's what you want, that's what we can do. I won't walk away. I won't be an asshole that leaves you behind. But I won't bond." He let out a sharp breath. "I can't, Jade."

There was something tortured in his words, and I understood. Maybe it wasn't about me. Maybe he wasn't rejecting me specifically. But I didn't want more than this. So I turned, my back pressed against the door as he trapped me between his arms. I sucked in a breath. He was naked, wet, and pressing against me.

"Deal." And then he crushed his mouth to mine.

I ran my hands down his back, feeling the scars. He tensed for an instant but kept kissing up and down my neck, tugging at my clothes.

For a wolf to scar like that, meant whatever had caused it had dug so deep into the skin that the wolves' regenerative powers couldn't heal it. I had seen a few scarred wolves, including one of the Healers of the Redwood Pack. That scar, much like the ones on his back, must have been made using a special salt or magic to remain that way.

Whoever hurt him had done it with the purpose to maim. So he would remember.

I kept my fingers touching his scars, letting fire dance along them.

He growled, and I knew he wasn't in pain. I had control of the flame. I could let him feel warmth, but I wouldn't burn him.

I didn't know why I was doing that, only that I needed to.

We had so many other problems on our path, we needed to work together, and I needed to stop fighting him.

But there had been a pull between us since the moment we met, and there was no stopping this.

He wanted this, just like I did.

He slid my shirt over my head, grateful he didn't tear it right off. Of course, I thought that too soon—he clawed off my jeans as if they were mere threads. His claws nearly dug into my skin, keeping me close.

"No bra?" he growled.

I shook my head and he lapped up my nipples, sucking and licking. I groaned, running my hands through his hair before he was down on his knees, slicing my panties with those same claws.

"You're going to owe me clothes."

"I can do that. But first, I need a taste." And then his hands were on my thighs, spreading me, and his mouth was on my pussy.

He ate me out, licking and sucking until I saw stars, coming on his face.

My knees went weak, and I tore into my magic, keeping me steady, but he continued to growl, licking and sucking until I hit a second orgasm right on the tail end of the first. That had never happened to me before. I was good at getting myself off. Very good at it. But apparently this wolf was better.

Damn him.

Or perhaps damn me.

He continued to suck, and lick, until I was on the floor, reaching for him.

I gripped him, my fingers not even reaching all the way around him, and I moaned, wanting him inside me.

I moved so he was on his back and I straddled his legs, rubbing my clit along his thigh as I wiggled down and took him in my mouth.

"Goddess, witch. Your mouth on me is like a wet heat that I can't stop wanting."

In answer, I licked at the tip, enjoying the way the barbell in the tip of his cock pressed against the roof of my mouth.

It must have been silver, burning at all times in order for him to keep the piercing through shifts, and it just made me hotter for him.

I wanted him, needed him, and I was so fucking happy that he was mine in this moment.

Flame tickled up my back, stretched along the seams that I had hidden for so long. I ignored it, pushing back my own magic.

This wasn't time for that.

"What was that?" Steele asked as he pulled me up

from his cock and held my shoulders. I hovered over him, needing, wanting, but terrified of the magic within me.

And that was the true secret. The true cost. Because I couldn't let anyone see.

"Magic. Mine."

"You're not just a fire witch, are you?"

I didn't nod, didn't shake my head. Didn't answer at all. Because no one could know my secret. No one was allowed to.

He just sighed and leaned up and kissed me.

It was a softer kiss than before, as if he were learning me. I didn't want that.

I didn't want him to see.

Perhaps I needed him to though.

"So many secrets, fire witch."

"You said we were just going to fuck, not share everything."

I straddled him as he slid his fingers along my jaw. "I guess not. We're not Pack, but we are lovers. And you are friends with my friends. Are you a danger to my Pack?"

My eyes flared then, and his grew gold with his wolf.

"Your Pack has nothing to fear from me. I am here to protect them. Whatever powers I hold, they are mine. Dara and Sawyer are part of this Pack, so I will protect them. With everything that I have."

And I will protect you before you walk away. Because they always walk away.

But I didn't say that. I couldn't.

"I don't want to have to fight you, Jade. Don't become my enemy."

"I could say the same for you. So let's finish what we started. And then we'll find the traitor, and we'll part ways. On friendly terms."

He slid his hands through my hair and tugged, the sensation making my pussy clench.

"That we can do." And then he crushed his mouth to mine and rolled us so I was underneath him. He lifted one leg up, so my knee was at my shoulder, and then he slid deep inside of me. No warning, no teasing, just hard and thick and long and deep inside me. I nearly came right then, my body arching, as he pinched at my nipples, twisting just on the edge of pain. Exactly what I needed. How did this wolf know exactly what I wanted and craved?

I didn't have time to think about it though, because he was moving, slamming into me as I scratched my fingernails down his arms.

"You can't hurt me," he growled, and I dug harder, flames pouring out of me. They didn't touch the room, nor him. Because I was in control, even as he sent me over the edge again and again. We twisted so I rode him, his hands on my breasts and my clit and everywhere else as I continued to move, his cock deep inside me.

Then I was on all fours, and he had his hands on my hips, digging deep into my flesh. I would bruise, and I would relish every single mark. He slammed into me from behind, and then his thumb moved in between my ass, pressing over my hole, until I groaned.

"That's it, take me." He used my own wetness as lube, and began to fuck me with his thumb, even as he fucked me with his cock.

It was all so much, too much sensation, too much everything. When I came again, he followed me, roaring like a lion, rather than the wolf he was. He hovered over me, teeth at my neck. He sucked and bit down, but didn't break the skin.

I froze, but he kept moving, continuing to fuck me through his orgasm.

"No mating mark. We can't do the mating mark."

He nodded against me, licking at the bruise that was sure to come.

Oh, he had marked me. And everyone would know by our scent that we had fucked.

But he hadn't done an actual mating mark.

To complete the bond between a wolf and their mate or mates, you had to do two steps. One was sex, which would complete the bond for the human. He had come inside me, no condom, no protection—because he couldn't get me pregnant, not when we weren't mates and not when I used my own herbs to protect against that. Wolves and witches didn't carry diseases. So we were safe there too. But it did lock into place one aspect of the mating bond.

But as long as he didn't mark me, and as long as the moon goddess didn't get any new tricks up her sleeve like she seemed to be doing as of late, we were safe.

I couldn't mate with him. Because I didn't trust myself or him. Not when the demon wanted me, not when I knew that Steele would walk away when things got tough. Because that's what they all did.

And if we were mated, the bond would move me directly into the Aspen Pack, and whatever magic was hiding the traitor would hide them from me as well. I needed to do what I did best.

I needed to be on the outside looking in so I could find them, protect my family and myself.

From my own choices, and from Steele.

When he slid out of me, I felt empty. I ignored the feeling.

Instead, I rolled to my back and let him hover over me, kissing me softly, finishing up as if we hadn't just changed our relationship.

I needed to break the tension. I needed this to be

nothing. I needed to continue to lie to myself so I could breathe.

Steele seemed to understand, because he smirked, looking way too sexy for his own good. "This time tomorrow?" he asked.

I laughed and just let myself be. "Because your wolf needs it?" I asked.

"Just as much as your fire," he teased.

I nodded before we went to the shower and cleaned up. I knew I was playing with fire, but in the end we would both get burned.

CHAPTER
EIGHT

Steele

CASSIUS'S HAND SLAMMED INTO MY CHEST, AND I
fell back, rolling to my feet swiftly, as I slashed out, not
using my claws since we were just training.

Cassius grinned at me. "Well, it seems that you're
getting slow in your old age."

I flipped off my friend.

"Seriously, you're getting slow. You better start
moving a little faster."

I did, knowing that Cassius was just pushing me
because I had been in a funk. He didn't know why, and I
wasn't about to tell him. Everyone else probably thought it

was the vampires and demon—the fact that we were in a literal war. They didn't need to know I was more worried about who I'd had in my bed the week prior. And who I couldn't stop thinking about. Nobody needed to know that.

I swiped out with my leg, taking Cassius out. He rolled to his feet, but I was there, taking him back down, my hand around his throat, claws at his belly. "Yield?" I asked, fangs out.

Cassius rolled his eyes, then slapped the ground. "Yield. You're mean when you're feisty."

I stood and held my hand out to help him up. Cassius clasped mine and stood. We rolled our shoulders back, shaking off the fight and readying to go again. "You call me mean, and yet you're the one who has been trying to egg me on by calling me old man. Not quite sure you have a leg to stand on."

"How about one more round," Cassius taunted, and I grinned before we went at it again. There were others standing on the sidelines, pausing their training to watch us.

Cassius was a lieutenant. And he could fight better than most. But I was the Enforcer. I had trained him. I knew all his moves, but then again, we had been friends so long he knew all of mine as well.

Fist over fist, kick by kick. We knew what we were

doing. I didn't mind the audience, they could learn a thing or two. Mostly from the other man, though. At least, that's what Cassius liked to boast.

We had been friends since childhood, when everything had been hell, and we'd been forced to hide who we were and who we fought for. When we hadn't been strong enough to take out an Alpha with bloated power thanks to dark magic.

By the time we were done, we were both sweaty and a little cut up because sometimes claws did happen, and laughing.

The fact that we could laugh at all when we were training to fight against beings stronger than us meant that we needed this far more than I had thought.

"Okay, you win," Cassius said with a laugh. I grinned and looked around to see Cruz stomping towards us.

"Did you hear that? He caved."

Cruz rolled his eyes and stared between the two of us. "You're covered in mud, some blood, and way too much sweat. I don't think your mate is going to be too happy to see you."

Novah came forward and smiled before she wrapped her arms around the very sweaty Cassius. "It's okay, I'm going to go throw him in the lake, and then clean him up."

"That's exactly what I like to hear," he said as he leaned down and pressed his lips against his mate's. They groaned into each other as if they were newly mated and hadn't been bonded to one another for years.

My wolf perked up at that, intrigued. I pushed away those thoughts because I didn't want to know what it would feel like to be connected to someone on that level. I couldn't. I had seen what happened when bonds were twisted, when you were forced to watch the person who was part of your soul die. I wouldn't do that. Not with my position as Enforcer. I was on the frontlines, I would throw myself in front of the Alpha. Our Alpha was a new father, one who had gone through so much hell that I was surprised he could even function on a daily basis sometimes. So I would do anything within my power to protect him.

I wouldn't want whoever was mine to stand behind and watch her life fade because she was connected to me.

And that was why Jade would never be mine. Let alone the fact that she didn't want to be mine. I held back a snort at that. No, she wanted nothing to do with me. Except for what we had in those few moments on the floor. Those moments that had been the hottest moments of my life. Not that I would let myself focus on that.

"I'm going to go on a quick patrol just to work out the kinks in my shoulders. Want to join?" Cruz asked, and I nodded, gratefully taking the towel from a maternal wolf who smiled at me. I wrapped my arm around her shoulders and hugged her tight as she sighed. A submissive wolf.

It wasn't anything sexual. It wasn't anything wrong, it was a submissive wolf needing a dominant for reassurance. Because she needed to take care of us, and I needed to protect. "Okay, now wipe the blood off your face. You're going to scare the pups."

I snorted at her tone. She was just as demanding as the dominant maternals. But that's what submissives did. I did as told, and smiled at her.

"Okay, what do you think?"

"You have a busted lip that'll heal soon, but you look as ugly as ever."

I snarled, just playfully, and though she still didn't meet my eyes because her wolf wouldn't let her, she laughed.

"There you go. All big and strong."

"I swear, aren't you supposed to cower before me?"

"Sure. Maybe tomorrow. I'll let you know."

She walked off to go help someone else, and I knew that she was on her break from training, as everyone needed to learn how to fight, at least to protect themselves and the pups. She was just here wanting to keep people safe because she could. Because she was that kind of person.

"Is she working with Audrey?" I asked as I pointed towards the young woman.

Cruz nodded. "Yep. You two have an eye for it. She'll never be a soldier, I don't think her wolf would let her, but she's on the verge of becoming a maternal submissive."

"I don't know if her wolf will let her do that either. But the sarcasm, that's good. She's not shy."

"We all come in our own shapes and forms. After all, she was right about you being ugly."

I flipped him off, and laughed when he pushed me, as we wrestled a bit.

"Didn't you just get cleaned up?" Audrey said as she came forward, folding her arms over her chest.

Cruz and I backed up from each other and held our hands up. "Sorry. We'll do better."

"Go for a walk and get out of here. You guys are both shirtless, wrestling around, and I need to keep everybody focused."

I looked down at myself and shrugged. "We're wolves. Nudity's nudity."

"You're a wolf, I'm a cat, but even if nudity is nudity, we're also still human."

"You just can't get enough of me, can you?" Cruz asked, and then laughed. "You know, I can't even joke like that anymore. It's really fucking cool to be mated."

Audrey beamed, looking as if some of the world that

she carried on her shoulders lifted just a little. "I know, right? It still surprises me each day."

"If you guys could stop waxing poetic nonsense about being mated, that would be great."

"Since you're the single one here, stop pushing around those pheromones and we won't have a problem."

"Shut up," I grumbled and turned to leave, ignoring Audrey's laugh.

"You doing okay? Your wolf had been riding high, but then you stopped for a bit. I figured you scratched an itch."

I snarled. "What is everybody's deal with wanting to know about each other's sex lives?"

Cruz just laughed. "First, you gave me so much shit when it came to Dara. You don't really have any say in what I'm doing right now."

"I have as much say as I want, damn it."

We moved through the forest, talking about patrols and life and Dara.

"You gave me so much shit for Dara, and I got it. I needed that. I needed the push." He paused, and I knew I wasn't going to like what came out of his mouth next. "You going to tell me what's going on between you and Jade?" he asked, and I bit my growl back, knowing that would say more than any words.

But then again, maybe my silence would do the same.

"Jade is my mate's best friend. I don't know what she went through or what secret she's hiding because we all have them, we all have our privacy, but there's something there. We can all tell."

"It's just attraction. It happens. Nothing more. You don't need to freak the fuck out."

He shook his head.

"I don't know if I believe you."

"I don't know if I care if you believe me or not."

"I get it. You don't want to talk about it. But if there's something there, maybe you shouldn't hide."

"And maybe you should mind your own fucking business."

Cruz held up both hands before his phone beeped and he pulled it out to look at the screen. "And well, my business, a.k.a. my mate, is wanting to see me."

From the way his eyes grew gold, I had a feeling I knew exactly why she wanted to see him.

"Seriously?" I asked, my voice deadpan.

"Seriously. But I don't mind. I'm going to go see what my mate wants, and I'm going to leave you to your thoughts. Maybe you should figure out what you want."

"What I want is to keep this Pack safe. And I can't keep doing that if my head is in the air or up my ass."

"That's a lovely visual."

Cruz took off and I watched him go, wondering what

the hell I was doing.

We were at war. We had a traitor, and I couldn't snuff them out.

Somebody who knew how we fought and knew how to get through the wards was weakening us one battle at a time.

And the problem was, we couldn't figure out who it was. I had spent months searching through the archives trying to find out how they could be using magic to hide their treachery within the bonds, but it didn't make any sense. We didn't have demonic history. The only ones who could help us were on the outside, and that meant Jade.

And that meant there was no escaping her.

And as if I had conjured her, there she stood. She looked like a powerful witch on a mission.

Her red hair flowed around her, looking like the fire she created and controlled. She looked healthier, as if she were finally healing. I still couldn't quite get the image of her nearly dying in my arms out of my mind, and I didn't know if I ever would.

Then again, I couldn't get the image of her coming in my arms out of my mind either. And I wasn't sure I wanted to.

"There you are," she said, and I raised a brow.

"You were looking for me?" I asked, and she rolled her

eyes.

"So sure of yourself. I didn't start the day looking for you. But then someone mentioned you were on a walk, and as I was overhearing it, I thought it'd be a good time to ambush you and talk."

I scoffed. "Oh, that sounds lovely. What's an ambush between—what are we, enemies? Friends? People who can barely stand each other?"

"Have you worked more on finding the traitor?" she asked, her voice low, deep and husky. It did things to me, and it made my wolf stand at attention. Of course, it wasn't the only thing standing at attention, not that I was going to let myself go there.

At least not right now.

"I'm trying to unravel the magic. It's so exhausting."

I stared at her, frowning. "Are you going to fucking hurt yourself doing this?"

She raised her chin. "I hope not. But magic takes work. I'm working on it. Just stop."

"I don't think I can."

"I want to know how the vampires are getting through the wards. Because I've seen the wards that your witches and Pack have built. They shouldn't be able to."

"Then somebody let them through," I bit out, revealing the one possibility that hurt more than anything. "I knew somebody was telling them our whereabouts, our plans. And I can't figure out who it is. But if someone is letting them through, to hurt our pups and cubs? I will gut the person. No matter who it is."

"And I'll help you."

"For a Pack that's not your own?" I asked without thinking.

She raised a brow. "I'm not Pack, you know why I'm not. If I were Pack, I wouldn't be able to see the magic from the outside. I would be obscured just like the rest of you."

"Fine," I bit out, knowing she was right and I was being surly for no reason.

"Are you just not going to touch me at all?" she asked, and I turned to her, surprised. "What?"

"I'm just trying to see where we stand. I like to be blunt. It helps."

My lips twitched, and I pushed her hair from her face, loving the way her mouth parted. "If that's what you want."

She laughed. "I was pretty sure that's what you wanted." She looked pointedly down at my crotch and my hard-on, and I shrugged. "Fun for now. Because we aren't a future."

I leaned down and pressed my lips against hers just because I could. "Nice."

She smiled. "I'm better than nice. Because I'm not

really nice."

"I'm not either. I'm an asshole for a reason."

"You're living up to that quite nicely."

I shook my head when suddenly my wolf went on alert and I whirled.

"What is it?" she asked, the powerful witch up at the forefront, and the sultry seductress pushed back.

"A breach."

I ran, Jade on my heels as I spoke into my communicator, alerting the rest of my team.

I was the Enforcer, I could sense it first, just like the Alpha, and I hoped I was quick enough.

"Oh my God," she whispered.

My sentiments exactly.

Three vampires stood at the edge of the wards, not quite past the wards, but had tossed a magical sensor against them. But that wasn't what shocked me. No, it was the human child in their arms.

The child was sleeping, its chest moving up and down as it breathed deeply, and I wanted to curse.

"What the hell?" Jade whispered.

"You should go. Get the others."

"You know they're coming, you just called for them. You can't keep me safe, but I can fight beside you."

I nodded as I looked at the vampire who seemed to be in charge.

"What do you want?" I asked.

"So many things," the vampire hissed. He leaned over and ran his finger over the plump cheek of the small child in the other vampire's arms.

My claws slid from my fingertips and I growled.

"You're going to hurt a child right in front of us? I could gut you before that happened."

"Perhaps. We'll just have to see."

The others weren't going to get there fast enough, not with the way the vampires were pushing at the wards.

I turned to Jade, and wished like hell we had a second bond like some wolves did. But all I could do was nod slightly. She raised her chin, and I had to hope she understood.

Then the vampires moved, and there were no more questions. No more answers.

It threw the child at us, which woke the baby up, screaming as it sailed through the air. I tore through the wards, Jade right behind me. She whirled out, burning one vampire, as I went at the other, clawing its face. I caught the still screaming baby in one arm before turning to Jade and handing over the child.

"Protect him."

"Steele!" she yelled as she cradled the baby close, and then a roar echoed in my head, and a vampire bit down, and there was nothing.

CHAPTER
NINE

Jade

"Wake up. Jade. Wake up."

"Jade. Wake up."

I fluttered open my eyelashes, ignoring the pounding in my temples.

I turned towards the sound of Dara's voice and frowned. "What happened?" I asked, coughing into my fist as I tried to sit up.

"No, lie back. Let us check on you."

Things came into full focus then, and I quickly sat up, ignoring Dara's curses. "I'm fine. I don't need anyone to look at me. Where is Steele?" I asked, looking around. "Where is he?"

Dara held my cheeks between her hands and frowned at me. "You aren't steady. What's going on?"

"Steele. Where's Steele?" I asked, pushing her hands off me. And then I remembered the attack, and the child.

The child.

I turned, heart in my throat, as Wren, our Healer, held the small child in her arms, checking the baby over for any wounds. The child seemed unharmed, if a little dazed. Considering I felt the same, I didn't blame the baby.

"They're safe."

"The vampires were here," I said, as I struggled to stand up, Dara's arm on my elbow keeping me steady.

"We saw that on the footage," Chase snarled as he came towards me.

I briefly met the Alpha's gaze, then lowered my eyes. I wasn't a wolf to try to play dominance games, but I also knew an enraged Alpha when I saw one.

"What exactly happened?"

"They sent one of their bombs towards us, and they had the child. Steele and I were close, so we did what we could."

The fire within me raged, the fire I couldn't let them know about. I did my best to ignore the magic that pulsed within me. The embers in my veins that threatened the world.

I was a fire witch, an elemental who could use fire. That was what I told the world. But only a few people knew the truth. And even those few didn't know the actual origin of my power.

And that power of flame and vengeance pushed at me, wanting out. Wanting revenge.

Wanting Steele.

"I don't know what they hit me with, but Steele saved the child, and I threw myself over the baby." I watched as the child was handed off to another Pack member through the wards. The baby would be safe and be returned to their human family.

I would heal, but I wasn't the only one here.

"They took Steele, didn't they?" I whispered the words in absolute rage.

They had threatened the Pack once again, and once again somebody had let them through.

"Whoever is on the inside working with the vampires knew exactly what they were doing," I spat, as Chase's jaw tightened.

"The traitor did this?"

"Yes. There's no other explanation. You guys have top-notch security, and you can always tell when a horde or a single vampire's coming towards you. You have technology and magic working together, and you can stop these skirmishes before they start. And yet, a human child and vampires were able to get this close to the wards, through the outer boundaries, and take Steele. Someone allowed that. Someone with knowledge." I looked around at the small grouping of people, the people that Steele trusted, and that fire within me blazed hotter.

"We need to find him. There was something about what they wanted him for." I shook my head, not wanting to think the worst, but knowing it might come.

"Where did they take him? How many were there?" Chase asked, and I pushed down the fire within and rubbed my temple. "There were three at first, then more. I don't know how many. Did you see anything on the recording?"

Chase cursed under his breath as the lieutenants came forward, and we tried to come up with answers.

Wren came over then, put her hand on my arm, and I shook my head. "I'm not bonded to the Pack. You can't Heal this headache away."

"I can give you something for the headache. It doesn't have to be magic. I'm also a trained doctor. I went to school and everything."

I'd forgotten that. I was so used to magic and the

bonds of Pack doing most of the work because whenever I saw Wren, we were in the midst of battle and there was blood and gore and death surrounding us. But, of course, she would also know how to help others.

"If she can't help, then I can," a familiar voice said from the trees, and everyone looked towards the voice. Of course, the shifters would've been able to scent Declan coming, but the witch who could manipulate metal probably knew that. He was arrogant, but not an idiot.

"Declan, what are you doing here?" I asked the coven member.

Declan had almost died numerous times in his life because of his power, and his uniqueness.

The coven before did not like anyone different. They only liked elementals they could control. When they were taken down years ago, it was because they had hunted those who were unlike them. Those who didn't believe in their righteousness. And then the coven had fixed itself, and new powers came forward, and people had been able to live freely as they were. I had even thought there was hope, which was odd for me because I didn't believe in hope most days.

Declan and Leta and Bishop and Dara and the ones we had lost along the way had all thought that perhaps we had a chance. It had been a small hope on my part, because I was not a team player. I had learned the hard way what happened when you relied on too many people. But I believed in Dara, and so when Dara had become an Aspen Pack member, I had waited.

I hadn't joined. Then Declan and Sawyer joined. Although Sawyer wasn't a witch, he was still powerful in strength of mind and loyalty.

In the end, the demon and Lily, the consort and traitorous bitch, had killed the old coven, and siphoned their power to bloat their own.

The siphon was a monster. Because you couldn't handle power not of your own.

A siphon could only hold onto power for so long. Eventually it would destroy them from the inside out, and it would take even darker magic to hold onto that. It became an addiction. Because that power would fade and they would need more and more.

So when Lily and the demon had taken all of the magic of the coven, performing the worst taboo of magic, as a dark magic user, she had sealed her fate.

I would kill her for daring to hurt those I loved. And now I would kill her for taking Steele.

He wasn't mine forever, but he was mine for now. And I did not share.

"The coven's here, we'll help you find him." Declan looked at me, then gestured towards the Alpha. "I know you didn't ask, but we are allies now. If you need us, we're there."

"And you just happened to be on your way here?" Cruz asked, and let out an oof as Dara elbowed him.

"I called them before Steele was taken, because we were all meeting to discuss how we could help in the first place. I just updated them. We're all friends now, so if you could stop antagonizing one another that would be great," Dara added.

My lips twitched, even though it was hard to find any humor in this moment.

"Yes. Let's all be friends. And find the fuckers who took him."

Gavin came forward, rubbing the back of his neck. "I might be the Tracker, and I can search along my bonds for him, but they're using some pretty dark magic to hide him from me."

"Then we use the magic of light to aid you," I said, as if it were obvious.

"Bishop and Leta are working with the wards, trying to seal up any holes," Dara explained, and I nodded at the mention of our other coven members.

"Good. They'll be good at that."

Leta was old, far older than she even told others, but she was also tired. I didn't know how she stayed so strong for all of us, but I had a feeling if we didn't let her rest at some point, it wouldn't be good for anyone.

And Bishop? Well, Bishop had his own reasons for wanting to stay away from the wolves. The fact that he was here at all was a testament to his own inner strength, even though he was more of an asshole than Declan and myself put together most days.

"Okay, I will use any help you can give me," Gavin put in. "Steele's alive," he said, and I pressed my lips together, the fire within me pushing. Because I needed to hear those words.

He wasn't mine. He wasn't my mate, and would never be. We had both been damn sure about that. But part of me wanted that bond just so I could keep an eye on him. That might make me crazy, but it was honest.

"Okay, find him. Bring him back, and try not to burn down the entire world when you do it," Dara said, death in her eyes.

Dara was a harvester death witch and had brought people back from death before. I wouldn't ask her to do that for Steele, because I knew there were consequences to every action. The vampires and demon would rue the day they decided to hurt him.

And I would deal with whatever that meant to me later.

❀

IN THE END, THERE WAS A SMALL GROUP OF US ON THE trail. It only took twenty minutes for us to gather our things and go. Gavin at the forefront, Declan at his side, the two of them using their magics in order to search for Steele.

I stood with Sawyer, as my friend hadn't wanted to be left behind. He had just raised a brow when I had asked why he would come.

I didn't know how he felt about Steele, but in the end, Sawyer was now an Aspen Pack member. It galled me that I hadn't even known. That he had put himself in harm's way to find me. To protect me. So, I would do whatever I could for him.

"Will you become a wolf?" I asked as we continued through the trees, searching for Steele or any evidence we could find.

Sawyer blinked at me, as did one of Steele's lieutenants as he walked past. Damn shifter hearing.

"I don't have any plans to. But I'm a member now. You never know."

"You have to be near death, and even then, with the bite and the claws and everything that comes from a very dominant wolf turning you, it doesn't mean you'll actually shift."

"That's true. It's not a high conversion rate, but it does happen. Ronan is a good example."

I nodded, thinking of the young man who had been turned by a rogue, and saved by the Aspens. The Aspens had almost been reprimanded by the US government for turning a shifter that wasn't Pack. But in the end Chase had said something to convince the president and senators who had been up in arms, doing what he did best.

He had protected his Pack. And now Ronan was safe, a newer member of the Aspen Pack and wolf that was learning his ways.

"You don't have to be magical in order to be an Aspen Pack member. Wynter is proof of that."

I nodded, thinking of the human woman who fought side-by-side with the others, training and learning to work with Chase so she was faster than any witch out there. But not as fast as a shifter.

"And you know, I could become a cat or maybe even a bear. It'd be fun to be a polar bear, don't you think?" he asked, speaking of the Omega who was the only polar bear I knew of in existence. In fact, the Aspens were the only Pack I knew with shifters other than wolves. The world was only just now coming to realize that there were other kinds of animal shifters. The wolves themselves and other Packs hadn't even realized. The former Aspen Pack Alpha had kept his secret because he had liked power, and Chase had continued to keep the secret to keep people safe.

"I can fight well as a human. I don't need to be magical in order to protect my friends. I have a purpose, Jade," Sawyer said softly. I reached out and squeezed his hand. The familiar argument between us not painful in the way it had once been.

Sawyer had saved me one day, when I had been lost in my own power, not able to protect myself. He had saved me because he had needed help, and it was easier to protect others than myself.

And we had been friends and confidants ever since.

There was no coming back from pain like that. No coming back from the power that overreached and took your soul.

And if I thought about the power within me, reaching out, tainted, it would overwhelm me. So instead I thought about who we needed to find, and how we would find him.

He had to be alive. Gavin kept telling us he was. As did Cruz, who had come with us. We had left Dara behind to shore up the wards and keep others safe, so Cruz was worried about his mate, and his friend, but we would find him. We had to.

"Something's different," I whispered as I stopped walking and looked around, feeling the fire within me dance along the inside of my skin. Sawyer froze and stared at me, the others realizing quickly that I had quit moving. They turned towards me, confusion on their faces, as I looked in a new direction.

"I don't know what's wrong, but there's dark magic there. Don't you feel it?"

Declan came forward, eyes narrowed. "Is it demonic? It's hard to tell."

"They're hiding Steele's location from me," Gavin growled. "I can't track him from here on. But if you're thinking the dark magic is that way, do we go towards it?"

"I don't think we have a choice," I whispered.

That song of fire crept up my body, aching, wanting more. And I knew I would have to move soon. I wouldn't have a choice.

A sense of urgency pulsed in my veins, and I began to run, ignoring the shouts from the others. Sawyer tried to pull me back.

They were there. I knew they had to be. I needed to fix this. Needed to stop it. Steele was there. We were going to be too late.

The others were at my side quickly. Did they sense the urgency that I did? The absolute horror that would come if we weren't fast enough?

We had to move. We had to get closer.

I burst through the trees into a clearing and froze, my blood throbbing, fire at my fingertips.

We were too late.

We had been too late.

Magic slammed at me and I threw up my hands, creating a wall of fire around all of us. Declan swore, then tossed out a coin, manipulating the metal into a barrier.

"Is that a fucking demon?" Declan asked.

I nodded, eyes wide. "It's the same demon who came at me. I would never forget his beautiful face."

"You're too late," the demon purred.

Lily stood at his side, looking radiant, and yet there was something in her eyes, something wrong.

Something was wrong with Lily. Beyond the fact that she had hated her place in the Pack so much she betrayed them.

Perhaps it was the fact that she was a siphon now. Always hungry for power but never getting enough.

Or perhaps it was just the fact that she was consort to a demon.

"I was hoping you would come, my firebird," the demon whispered, and I froze.

Did the others know? Did they know what that word meant?

No, they couldn't.

But the fire within me burned, wanting more, wanting

to touch. It wanted that demonic fire that surrounded him. Like called to like.

I wasn't a demon, wasn't bonded to one or blooded by one. I was a witch with the power of fire, but I also had demon fire—the firebird.

It was what others called a monstrosity, what others cursed to hell.

I contained that power within me because I refused to let it break. I refused to become the siphon Lily had become.

I looked between the two of them, past the vampires that stood ready to fight us all, the dozens waiting for their master to order them to slaughter us.

And I looked at the kneeling man between them.

Steele was shirtless, cuts all over his body. His eye was blackened and bruised and swollen. He had burns and slices all down his flesh, and his arms were tied with magic in front of him. Steele continued to fight the bonds, pushing at them, trying to get free.

Those were demonic shackles. Even worse than the ones that had kept me down.

I met his gaze, saw the anger and the determination. I would not let him die here. I would save him just like he had saved me.

I met Declan's gaze and he nodded, and then the wolves howled and attacked.

The demon seemed to have been waiting for this moment, because he laughed and the vampires moved as one.

We were far outnumbered, but we were strong.

I slammed out a wave of fire towards a dozen vampires. They screamed, going to their knees. Declan buried them in metal, while Sawyer stabbed his way through, the wolves that had come with us barreling their way through with teeth and claws.

And I kept moving, my eyes only on Steele.

I just had to get through.

Then the demon moved and slid his hand along Steele's shoulder. He squeezed, and I kept moving, slamming out fire, letting the firebird come closer to the surface than I'd ever let her before.

"And now he's mine, isn't he?" the demon asked softly, as he knelt down and bit directly into Steele's neck.

Steele's body bucked and he screamed, an unearthly scream that never should have been ripped from his lips.

Shock slammed into me and I kept moving, knowing I was far too late.

It was all far too late.

When the demon cut his palm I reached out, throwing firebomb after firebomb at him. But Lily used her stolen magic to deflect me, one blow after another. But

I ignored her and kept going, using every ounce of power and magic I had in me. I had to stop him.

The demon bite wouldn't be fatal, it couldn't be. But what the demon was planning next would.

The demon dripped a single drop of blood from his cut palm onto the open wound at Steele's neck.

And the world shattered.

CHAPTER
TEN

Steele

WITH EVERY BREATH, I FOUGHT.

Darkness, fire, anger.

Despair.

It was all there, it had to be. It pushed at me, clawing into my flesh as if it were the demon from my nightmares, not the demon that stood behind me.

I fought at my bonds, but the magical chains seemed to dig into my skin with each passing moment. As if the harder I fought, the tighter I was bound.

They had taken me from my home because I saved a child. I tried to save Jade. Now Jade was running towards me, flames in her hands, and I wasn't going to be able to save her. Maybe if I was lucky, she would save me.

I wasn't too proud to be saved. If somebody could help me out of this, I would appreciate it. Because I did not want to die here, screaming for my mother.

Even though those words weren't ripped out of me, that's all I could hear.

That familiar refrain of a memory.

I screamed for her once, and she hadn't broken free.

I screamed for my father, but he hadn't broken free.

Instead, I had watched their heads roll towards me, abject fear on their faces.

I watched it all, and I screamed. And it was the same scream that ripped from my throat today.

Icy fire dug deep into my shoulder where the demon had bitten, and I knew what this had to be. I knew what this had all been about. They wanted hybrids. They wanted their next phase of evolution.

And this monster wanted me to be it.

Well, fuck that. I would fight. I wouldn't hurt my Pack. I wouldn't become a liability.

I pulled my arms up, ignoring the way that the bonds against me felt as if I were breaking each bone little by little, sawdust and powder the only thing left.

I could hardly breathe, but I had to try. I had to get out of this.

I would not die like this.

I couldn't die like this.

And then the demon bit down again. I fought, I pushed, I clawed. It was as if there was a film over my eyes, it was hard to figure out exactly what was going on.

Only Jade was there, bowling down vampires with fire as if she had been doing this for a thousand years. She moved with a grace I had never seen before. As if there was something else propelling her. The fire in her eyes danced blue and then purple and then white, before sliding back into reds and oranges. It wasn't the fire I was used to seeing, but she seemed to still be in control, moving towards me. The horror on her face though reminded me that this could be the end.

The demon wanted me as its hybrid. But it wasn't going to be like before. No, this was going to be something new. Something I didn't know if I was going to be able to control.

I pushed at my bonds again, but the demon slammed into me, trying to knock me out.

I couldn't tell what was happening, couldn't tell what I needed to do.

The demon was gone, and so was Lily.

The traitor was gone, and I couldn't breathe. Couldn't focus.

I watched my friends fight through the horror that

were these vampires, and it was as if there was no return. No way to stop this.

When they took me, they knocked me out. By the time I awoke, they had already etched runes onto my skin for whatever ceremonial engravings they needed. They had cut some into my skin, but my wolf had tried its best to heal.

Now my wolf was howling, trying to push us both through.

I would not let my wolf die for this. I would not let any of us die for this.

And then something changed.

Jade was still running towards me, still fighting through vampires. Sawyer was there, slicing them up as quickly as he could, moving so fast for a human, but not fast enough. Not fast enough to get to me.

I was on my own.

Another scream ripped from my throat, but I couldn't even hear it.

Because there was something new inside me, a beast. A monster.

Was this what a hybrid was? A monstrous being that just plowed through his friends and killed innocents?

I couldn't let that happen. I fought and pushed down whatever was telling me to kill my friends.

But it whispered.

Change who you are.

Cut them. Gut them. They are meat.

Serve your master.

I ignored it. I ignored everything that it was saying, but it kept growling at me. And it was strong. I had to fight back.

My hands changed into claws, and they were wolf, but then they slid back into human. I was shaking, sweat pouring down my body and mixing with the blood already there.

I had to fight, I had to fight this.

And then my friends were there.

Cruz grabbed ahold of me, keeping my head still, as Sawyer rinsed off the blood with water he had in his flask.

Gavin was yelling into a phone, my lieutenants surrounding us, creating a perimeter.

And then Jade was there.

The monster inside me bucked, trying to get to her. My hands were free, someone having removed my restraints and I hadn't even noticed.

I reached out to Jade and tried to wrap my hands around her neck, before I realized what I was doing and pulled back.

But she didn't stop hovering.

"You're going to be okay," she whispered.

Was she whispering or yelling? I didn't know. I couldn't tell.

It felt like everything was happening all at once and I couldn't keep up.

"What's happening to me?" I asked.

"You're going to be fine," Cruz said as calmly as he could, but I didn't believe him.

"Liar," I snarled, as the beast within me pushed again, wanting more.

It wanted everything, and I had nothing to give it.

It wanted me to kill my friends, to go back to that den and kill everyone in sight. Something was controlling me, and it wasn't me.

I was the Enforcer.

My eyes widened as the ramifications hit home.

"The bombs. You have to kill me, kill me!" I screamed at Jade.

Cruz bucked behind me, as if I had hit him.

Gavin cursed and Sawyer just looked sad.

But Jade cupped my face and shook her head.

"I can help. I can help!"

"Kill me. Please. If I'm a hybrid," I gasped, blood spewing from my mouth as I said it. "If I'm a hybrid, it could hurt the bonds. I'm the Enforcer. I protect the Pack. Help me protect the Pack."

My hands were claws now, but they were not my own.

I had never seen them before.

I was changing, and I couldn't stop this.

I needed to stop this.

"You can't. You can't."

"I'm never going to kill you. That will not happen. But I can help you, Steele. I can help you but you have to do the one thing you know I would never ask you to do."

"What?" I snarled, as everyone else stared at her.

She looked around and then cursed.

"Go. Leave us. I need privacy for this."

"Fuck no, Jade."

She looked at her friend then, at Sawyer, who stared wide-eyed at her.

"You know what I need to do. Just tell the others. We need—I need space. Please."

I was shaking beneath her hold, but I didn't move.

I had enough control for this. I needed enough control for this.

And for some reason, they believed her.

They believed she could control me.

It was that, or let me die.

Because we didn't have another option.

They moved to give us space and keep the area secure, or fight other vampires, or whatever else needed doing. Jade had pushed my hair back from my face as I gritted my teeth and tried to breathe.

"You have to do the one thing I said I would never ask," she repeated.

"What?" I snarled.

"Mark me. Bond with me. My power can stop this, can help you find control. I promise you."

"Are you fucking kidding me?" I asked, trying to sit up.

She didn't stop me, instead she sat next to me, pushing my hair back from my face as I tried to maintain control.

I was human, for now, I could feel it.

We were tucked behind trees, somehow hidden, but still too far in the fucking open.

"I'm bonded to the Pack, Jade. I'm going to kill everybody if I go back."

"I'll help you with control. I promise. I'll never let you hurt your friends and family. I'll never let you hurt *my* friends and family. So let me do this. Let me protect you." There were tears streaming down her face.

I had never seen Jade cry before. She was always so strong, so sarcastic; this was something new.

It almost felt like a trick I didn't understand.

"I need the mating bond with you, and then I can calm the beast. I promise."

For some reason, that made me laugh, and I had to fight for control again.

"Did you just make a sex joke?" I asked.

"Just do it," she said. "Mark me and make me yours. I'll save you."

"You've lost your fucking mind."

She pressed her lips to mine, hard and fast, and it was as if my wolf reached out, begging.

It knew its mate, it knew what needed to happen.

"I'll kill you."

"You won't. I promise. But if you don't control your beast right now, and I'm not talking about your wolf, you will die. But I can stop it. I promise you."

My wolf howled and I gave in.

I pounced.

Knowing I had probably just killed us both.

CHAPTER
ELEVEN

Jade

MY BACK HIT THE HARD GROUND WITH A RESOUNDING thwack, and yet his hands on my hips, on my shoulders, took the brunt of it somehow. Even in this craze, the three parts of him fighting for dominance and control in a haze of fire and torment, he was still protecting me.

Because that was Steele.

The Enforcer who refused to let anyone in, to let anyone see who he was, yet threw himself bodily to protect everyone in his care.

That was what had attracted me to him the moment I saw him, when he had come to find Cruz and Dara all those months ago. The moment we'd looked into each other's eyes and known.

Oh yes, I had known in that instant he could be mine. I wasn't a shifter. It wasn't as if I could sense a potential bond that didn't yet exist that the moon goddess had chosen him for me.

No, there was something else inside me, a fiery ember that screeched for its other half.

I didn't get that future. I hadn't gotten it when I was rejected the first time. And I wasn't going to allow myself to go through that again. And yet, in that instant when he held me and crushed his mouth to mine, I knew there was no other choice.

To save him, I would give him part of myself.

Because I was the firebird. I was magic and fire and earth and danger. I held within me a beast of my own. A monster that no one who knew of it spoke of. I could control the fire of demons. I was born that way, and I would die that way. I held no drops of demon blood within me. I wasn't a hybrid, I wasn't of hell. But my power was the counter to hell, though not everyone could see that. Not everyone would believe that.

So I kept it hidden. Because to control it was to let go of part of myself. And I had always vehemently refused to be that.

When I nearly died all those years ago, almost

taking Sawyer with me, we had grown close because of it. I taught Sawyer to protect himself with spells, using his own innate human magic—his soul—to protect himself.

He wanted to protect me, to protect our people, but it hadn't been enough. He hadn't had enough within him because he wasn't meant to protect everyone, which was why he became an Aspen.

So many choices, so many chances, all culminating in this moment—Steele's mouth on mine, and my inevitable surrender.

He pulled back, looking at me with wide eyes. I could see the human, this was Steele. But when he blinked it was the wolf, gold and menacing and scared. His wolf was so scared.

And then it went gray, the hybrid, the monster the demon wanted to unleash upon the world and send to start an apocalypse.

This was the beginning, but wouldn't be our ending.

I gripped his face, keeping him steady.

"It's okay. You won't hurt me," I lied.

Because Steele would never physically hurt me. Even in the state where three beings warred, where the battle for dominance possibly meant true death, he wouldn't hurt me.

But giving in to that, trusting somebody with the other

half of my soul, would bare me to the endless hurt that came with loving someone else.

Because I had loved someone else before, and they had broken me. And nearly everyone else in my life that I tried to protect, nearly everyone else I tried to love, died.

But I couldn't let Steele die. He deserved so much more than the agony embracing him, or the death coming for him.

So I would use the power I hid, the power I suppressed, to protect him.

"Just complete the mating. You have to complete the mating."

"Can't." A growl. "Hurt you."

He struggled through each word, the veins in his neck throbbing.

He was already shirtless, his pants in tatters, so I tugged on my own shirt, wiggling out from it as he hovered over me, his claws digging into the ground.

The others would be able to hear us. They were shifters with keen hearing. They would know exactly what was going on. But I didn't care. This wasn't a show, this was sacrifice and survival.

And this was a man I craved. I was going to let that be enough for now. I would deal with the consequences when it wasn't literally life-or-death.

If that moment ever came.

"Jade. I'll hurt you. You should go."

"I already told you you're not going to hurt me. Let me help you. Let me do this. Let me save us."

"This is forever," he growled, his fangs sliding out of his gums.

I nodded tightly, and then there were no more words.

He crushed his mouth to mine again, and I let him, and I just let myself be in the moment.

The magic within me burned, wings pressing under my skin, waiting.

His eyes were closed, he couldn't see them anyway once they peeked around my back, but he would soon. There would be no hiding who I was, what I could do.

But that was why we were doing this. So I could use who I was to protect him.

His claws dug into the side of my pants, pulling them down, and I was grateful that he didn't tear them to shreds. I didn't have any spares anywhere close. His lips never left mine, his hands running up and down my body. I tugged off his pants and gripped him tightly, leading him to me.

"Fast. I'm ready," I whispered.

"No, you're not," he growled, and then with the presence of mind no hybrid would have, but was all Steele, he kissed his way down my body, taking extra time on my breasts, biting and sucking until they were hard little points, before he knelt between my legs and licked me.

I arched off the ground as his tongue delved between my folds, sucking on my clit. He bit down gently, his fangs scraping against my sensitive skin, and I groaned at the danger.

He could mark me there, for no one to see but us, but he wouldn't. No, he would wait until he was buried balls deep inside me.

And when he speared two fingers inside me, I came, clamping around him, my body rocking along the hard ground.

I tugged on his hair, but he lapped at me some more before he licked his way back up my body and kissed me again.

I reached between us and guided him towards my entrance.

"Finish the bond. You have to."

I saw it in his eyes then, the precipice that he stood upon. He would lose control if we weren't careful, and so we would do this for each other. What we had to do.

And with one last look, he plunged deep inside me.

I groaned at the hard intrusion of his entrance.

He was long and thick and stretched me. I leaned into him, meeting him thrust for thrust as he pounded deep inside me. He was beautiful, sexy, and would break me if I wasn't careful.

But then again, I could break him just as easily.

He pulled one of my legs up, knee up to my shoulder, and pounded hard, jackknifing into me. This was all wolf. His claws dug into my flesh, but not breaking skin. He was still careful enough for that, and I knew if I wasn't careful, I might fall for my mate.

Maybe that wouldn't be so bad, but this wasn't a choice either of us were truly making. It was a choice thrust upon us and we were leaning into it.

So there would be no emotions, there would just be salvation. Endurance.

His fangs slid out of his gums again as he lowered my leg. I wrapped my legs around his waist and tilted my neck to the side.

"Mark me. Complete the bond."

He met my gaze again, and his eyes went from their normal green, to gold, to gray. Three souls trapped in one, three warriors fighting for dominance.

The hybrid could be tamed, I knew it in the depths of my soul. This was why I had been created, why I had fought so hard against the magic within me.

I would save the man, protect the wolf, and tame the beast.

Somehow.

He plunged and I came apart, my body arching into him. He lowered his head, his mouth to my shoulder, and bit.

I screamed at the pain, just a sharp pulse of red-hot agony as he bit into my neck. He marked me as his, blood flowing from the wound, but he didn't tear, he didn't rend. He marked me with such delicateness, I knew that whoever was in control then didn't want to harm.

The bond snapped into place and he came inside me, two halves of the mating bond tethered together.

But this wasn't a normal mating bond. This was a choice, one we were making, but one of different magics blending together.

The wolf and human of him clamped onto the bond, and I could sense his soul willing the rest of him to lean in and to never let go. The witch and human part of me leaned forward and gripped tightly as well, holding on for dear life. The goddess would want this, the goddess needed this. And so did I.

We both shook, connected together in body and soul and hope. When his eyes met mine, I saw the fear there.

But we were mated, I could sense his heartbeat along the bond.

Thump. Thump. Thump.

Steady but fearful an powerful.

He was my mate, and there was no breaking this, no going back.

Another bond slid into place, wrapping itself around me, but I ignored it.

I knew what that was, and I would have to deal with it. We would all have to deal with consequences later.

I just looked up at him and brushed his hair from his face. We laid there, locked together, holding one another. Sweat slick, out of breath, and I couldn't help but wonder what the fuck just happened.

"Steady, Steele. Steady," I whispered.

He looked at me then and his eyes went gray. A dark gray that scared me more than words could ever utter.

He pulled out of me and threw himself a good ten feet away.

I scrambled up, sore, naked, my hands outstretched.

"You're fine, you're safe."

He shook his head, and I let myself breathe for the first time today.

"I will protect the bond. We will protect it."

I let out a breath and let my wings unfurl.

They were of fire, mesmerizing in their beauty. That was what my mother had said before she perished in front of me.

Steele knelt in front of me, naked, his body rippling as it threatened to shift into a hybrid or wolf, or maybe a monstrous combination of both, if we didn't find a way for him to control it.

But my firebird was strong enough for that.

My wings fluttered, fire and flame and ash. He was mesmerized, watching as I beat my wings once, twice. The magic engulfed the bond, I could sense it running along the thread that connected us before slamming into him.

Steele's gaze went gray again and he knelt on all fours, ready to rush at me.

But I beat my wings again, pushing as much strength as I could towards him.

Again and again he fought, but I was stronger in this.

Because I had to be.

Because Steele needed me to be.

He had saved me once, he continued to save me every day.

I would do this for him.

I stepped forward, one foot at a time, my wings beating, when he shifted.

I sucked in a shocked gasp as he shifted to a hybrid form. His body steel-gray, heavily muscled, part wolf, part human—a monstrous combination of both.

He threw his head back and howled, calling the others back to the clearing, eyes transfixed.

"What the hell?" Cruz asked, and I held out my hands.

"Let me finish."

I didn't know if they were more shocked at seeing both of us naked, the fact that I had fiery wings, or that Steele was now a hybrid.

It didn't matter. Because I had to fix this.

I beat my wings again and he howled, body shaking, as he moved towards me, claws outstretched.

The demon wanted him to kill me. The demon controlling him wanted Steele to do the unthinkable.

But I was stronger. Steele was stronger.

And Malphas would rue the day he dared to ever fucking hurt us.

Steele crept towards me until his eyes went gold and he howled again, this time shifting from the monstrous form back into wolf. Bones broke, blood splattered, and I let tears finally fall as I watched the pain in his eyes as he shifted back to wolf, and then human again, then back to hybrid, then wolf. The others came forward, the look of agony on their faces mirroring mine in horror, until Steele finally crawled forward, human, covered in blood and who knew what else, and reached out to me with his hand.

"Jade," he gasped, and I went to my knees and held him. He crushed me in his arms and I held him close. The others began to talk but I shushed them, waving them away. They wouldn't go far, and I heard the truck come closer, knowing that we would be safely taken away, safely taken back to the Healers in the Pack. I just held him.

"You are safe. You're strong. My fire can save you."

Steele looked up at me with agonized eyes, and through cracked lips, whispered, "Did I hurt you?"

My heart broke again, because this wasn't how a mating was supposed to start. This wasn't how you were supposed to fall for the one who was supposed to be yours forever.

I shook my head. "No. You didn't."

And it wasn't a lie. He wouldn't. He couldn't.

"You're stuck with me," he whispered, and it was like a blow to my chest. I nodded tightly against him.

"Same here," I said, putting as much sarcasm into my voice as possible. From the way Sawyer and Cruz looked at me, I knew they heard the falseness of my tone, knew what I was trying to do.

But it didn't matter.

Because I had no idea what we were going to do, and from the way Steele sagged in my hold, he didn't either.

We were well and truly mated. With no takebacks.

And Steele, the Enforcer of the Aspen Pack, was now a hybrid.

The Aspen Pack was well and truly fucked.

CHAPTER
TWELVE

Steele

It was odd. I was born with a shifter inside me. A wolf soul I shared a body with.

Eons ago, when the first shifter was made, it was because of a murder. A human hunter had killed with such glee, with such vengeance, that he was punished.

The moon goddess had walked amongst the humans, pain in her heart as she knelt down in front of a dying wolf, its furred head cradled in her arms. She hadn't been able to save him, not directly. But out of vengeance, out of that horrible pain from losing a soul, she had done the unthinkable in some others' eyes.

She'd created a shifter.

She'd taken the soul of the wolf, its body long past saving, and placed it inside the human. The human had screamed and begged. From there, he had been forced to learn how to survive within a body that contained two souls, the wolf and the human fighting for dominance, fighting for control. It had been a curse in his eyes, the moon goddess's punishment.

But it wasn't. It couldn't be.

And out of rage and a sense of belonging, that man had created the three triplets, the three brothers, the original shifters.

In the end, they were the direct ancestors of the Talon Pack, although most people didn't know that. Those three created shifters spread throughout the world and congregated into Packs. Those Packs had hierarchy, with more magic from the moon goddess. She created her children and needed to protect them.

The sun goddess had created the cats in her image, and the midnight goddess had created the bears.

I didn't know the history of the sun or midnight goddesses, or what led them to create their children.

Some amongst us had even heard the moon goddess's voice as she did her best to protect us. But there was only so much a goddess could do in these times. They no longer walked among us, were no longer prayed to. They lived on another plane, just like the demons. But while the demons had slid through, and Malphas created vampires, the moon goddess sacrificed part of herself to protect us.

We were stronger now, had a greater connection to ourselves and our wolves because of her. The way that matings had changed was due to the sacrifice of the moon goddess. The fact that our wards were now a culmination of magics not just of our own was also due to the moon goddess.

And so while I knew she had blessed me as the Enforcer, one who could protect our Pack, I wasn't only hers anymore.

There was a third soul—no, perhaps not a soul. But a third beast.

I was now a hybrid.

Connected to earth, the goddess, and hell.

Wren stood in front of me, my Healer, a lynx shifter so submissive it was sometimes hard for her to even look into our gazes, and sighed. She didn't bother averting her gaze from me now. The strength within her allowed her to move past that submissiveness. I saw the pain in her eyes.

"I don't think you can fix me, Doc," I said gently, trying to put humor into it, but I didn't think I was successful.

There was no humor that could fix this.

"You're healthy. You're good. There's just something

more within you. And whatever Jade is doing, it's helping you keep control of it." Wren pushed her hair back from her face again and began to pace. I watched the movement, rubbing my hand over my chest.

She had healed my wounds, had found a way to connect to all parts of me, all parts of my soul, so she could heal the bruises and the cuts and whatever internal bleeding I had from the fight.

But there was no healing away whatever the demon had done to me.

I would be forever scarred in ways no one could see.

"I'm a liability," I growled, but it was Hayes who growled back, not Wren.

The polar bear shifter frowned at me and shook his head. I could sense him trying to reach towards me along our bond as Omega and Enforcer. He wanted, no *needed*, to protect me. To soothe the emotions deep inside. But I was just as stubborn as always, and from the look in his gaze, Hayes understood.

I stared over at Hayes and shook my head. "There's nothing you can do."

"That sounds like a challenge," the big polar bear said, running a hand over his hair. He stared at Wren, then sighed. "There's something I can do. I can ease your burden."

I shook my head. "You can't stop the hybrid. Nobody can. It killed everyone else."

"It hasn't killed you," my Alpha said from the doorway as he walked into my room.

We were in my house, after having been at the Healer's clinic for the first few hours. Then it had been too much for my wolf and whatever the hell was inside me and I had wanted to go back to the familiar. The comfortable.

The others had joined and had agreed that I did need to be comfortable. And known.

Jade was in the other room, talking with Sawyer and the others. I could sense her along the bond, that new bond that scared the fuck out of me.

How had I ended up mated?

My fucking mate was in the other room and I could sense her there. A slight pulse along the bond that calmed my wolf.

It made no fucking sense to me that this was true. That this was my life.

I hadn't expected this. I hadn't known that it could be like this.

I had never wanted a mate. Had never wanted that responsibility. I already had enough fucking responsibility on my shoulders. I didn't need the possibility of watching my life end if I lost her. Because whoever was mated to the Enforcer, just like the Alpha, would be in constant danger. That was just how things were.

One of my friends from the Redwoods, one of the main Enforcers there, had lost his first mate in a vicious and brutal attack. He lost part of himself and had nearly destroyed everything in the process.

He had been mated to his second mate now for over thirty years. They were steady, strong.

But I still saw the pure terror in his eyes whenever he was looking at his mate and he thought no one else would see.

Because even after all these years, he was so damn afraid of losing her.

He loved his mate. They had children and grandchildren now. He also still loved his first mate, the one who was gone for so long that even though people still spoke of her, not everybody remembered her.

I didn't know what I would do if I lost Jade, and I didn't even know her well enough to love her.

I could fall in love with her. And that was the problem. My wolf craved her, and so did I.

And the beast? That hybrid? It wanted her too.

For the connection, for the calm? Or because it was now part of me, and I knew that I was irrevocably altered by being mated to Jade.

She was the firebird, which I still had no idea what

that meant, was something I had never heard of, and she was strong.

But I didn't know if she was strong enough to survive. Not when the demons and vampires out there wanted to kill her. And I wasn't sure if I was the one strong enough to survive if I lost her. Maybe that was the crux of it—that I didn't know who I would become. *What* I could become.

"You steady now?" Chase asked, and though he phrased it like a question, it wasn't one. He was downright ordering it, and I was fine with that.

It didn't make any sense that I had survived, that the demon had done something to me, but for now at least I was grateful.

Grateful when I didn't even know how the hell I had ended up here.

"Come on up to the living room, we have to talk," Chase ordered, and turned and left. I had seen the wolf in his gaze, though I hadn't met those eyes for long. No, the Alpha was fucking pissed, and I was right there with him.

"What do you say, Doc, am I fit for whatever the hell's about to happen next?"

Wren looked past me towards the open door where the Alpha had just been and sighed. "I don't think any of us are. But you're healthy. And that's saying something considering I was terrified that you had just been killed. I'm glad you're not dead. We like you. And your mate."

She smiled as she said it before she moved out of my reach and followed the Alpha.

Hayes sighed and stared at me. "Let's not fuck this up, shall we?"

"What?" I snapped.

"You're good at pushing away people you like. People that like *you*. You're mated now. You don't get to do that anymore."

With that all-too-knowing and annoying comment, he left. I followed, knowing that we were on a precipice.

I wanted to be near my mate. I hadn't even realized I was moving towards her until I stood next to her and brushed my arm against hers. She raised a single brow but didn't comment.

Everyone stared at us, as if wondering what the hell we were going to do, and I wasn't sure either.

Did I lean down and kiss her? Did I hold her hand? Did I do anything?

This was a war council. A meeting to figure out what the fuck we were going to do against this demon, and yet all my wolf wanted to do was move forward, brush against her, and claim her again.

She carried my mark. Everyone could see it and scent it. But I wanted to reinforce it.

If this was the damn mating urge, no wonder wolves went fucking insane at the beginning of mating.

I was stronger than that. At least I had to pretend I was just then.

Nobody spoke, and I could sense they were intrigued, and yet also wanted to give us privacy. But there was no time for that. There was no time for anything.

Instead, I ran my knuckle against her cheek, sating my wolf, before I sat down on the couch behind us. Jade studied my face before she nodded and sat down next to me.

And with that, Chase let out a breath and began. "How the hell did the traitor get in here? And what the hell are we going to do about it?"

Cassius cleared his throat. "I don't know. We can't see anything from the cameras, or sense anything through the wards. Whatever this person is doing, they're careful about it. They're getting in undetected and finding our weakest points."

"Well, fuck that. I'm tired of watching our people get hurt, of watching us change everything that we are in order to protect ourselves," Audrey snapped. Gavin held her hand and nodded silently with her.

"The demon is changing everything. He's breaking us from the inside out and making it so we can't even use the protections we have from the goddess to protect ourselves. What the hell are we supposed to do with that?" Gavin snarled.

"I don't like this at all," Skye whispered. She didn't have her child with her, as the baby was with her grandparents over in the Redwood den. I knew it must have been hell on both of them, but she would be safer with the Redwoods than us for now.

The fact that I could even think that broke me.

I was the Enforcer. It was my job to protect us from outside forces. But there was something inside, a danger that I couldn't sense.

"If we used dark magic like the demon, we'd be able to sense the traitor," Dara began, then held up her hands as the wolves and shifters in the room growled.

I knew where Dara was going, I could sense it because Jade was so in tune with her best friend that it sank along the mating bond so I could see past the intense rage at even considering dark magic. It was odd, because this wasn't how I did anything. This wasn't me. I was changing —from the hybrid, from Jade, from the choices that had been thrust at us. And I didn't fucking like it.

"She's not saying that," Cruz snapped. "She's saying that if we went through dark magic and sacrificed and killed our loved ones in order to protect the others, we'd be able to find it. But we're not going to do that, so we have to be smarter. We have to find a way around it."

Dara smiled at her mate and nodded. "Exactly."

"What about the witches, can the coven help?" Wynter asked.

I was no longer surprised that Wynter was there. She wasn't a member of the hierarchy, but she was a human who had connections that we didn't. We needed people from all sides of this, with different experiences to help us through. She brought a vulnerability that the others didn't have. Because her lifetime was shorter, her weaknesses were in the forefront, and she hid her strengths. We needed her, and I was damn proud of how far she had come.

"I can't sense who it is," Novah said as she held onto her mate Cassius's hand. "I'm a Truth Seeker. I can sense the truth that people are speaking, but with this demon's magic embedded into our Pack, it's like it was with Blade again."

I no longer flinched at Blade's name, neither did Chase. And I was grateful for it. Because when we feared that name, when we feared those memories, we couldn't move forward. And yet, I still wanted to rage at the thought that our foundations were based in blood and hatred. How else were we supposed to move forward?

"It has to be someone that is close to us, someone that knows what we're doing, and I hate that," Chase murmured.

"Could it be somebody that doesn't know they're a traitor?" Jade asked, and I turned to her, eyes narrowed.

"What?" I snarled.

She squeezed my hand and didn't flinch at the growl in my tone. Hell, what was I supposed to do with a mate? I had never prepared for this, and Jade didn't back down from me. I was the asshole, the one who pushed others around to make sure that they could protect themselves. And Jade didn't back down from me. What was I supposed to do with this?

"All I'm saying is if we can't sense who is betraying us to Malphas and the others, perhaps it's for a reason. Perhaps they don't know what they're doing. At least not consciously."

Chase snarled and began to pace, Skye looking up at him, worry etched onto her features.

The people in this room were my best friends. Humans and wolves and witches and other shifters that I would die for. They had all bled to protect each other and me.

The thought of someone in this room, or one of my lieutenants, or one of the new recruits being a traitor curdled everything in my stomach.

But my wolf could not sense who the traitor was. It was being blocked not only by dark magic, but perhaps something unknown.

"I have to go through things again, try to figure it out. There's a taint within our bonds, and we can't survive if we don't figure out who it is."

Jade nodded and squeezed my hand. "I know I've been staying here for many reasons and one of them was to sense who the traitor was and try to slide around the demon magic. But now things are different."

She looked at me, and I cursed under my breath as everything started to click.

"Shit."

Her mouth twitched into a small smile before she sighed, and everyone began talking at once.

"What, what's going on?" Gavin asked.

"I'm Pack now." She laughed when everyone stared at her, comprehension finally hitting. "I guess we missed that when I mated in, didn't we?"

"Fuck. You're being blocked now too, just like us. You're not going to be able to use whatever magic you have. That firebird that I don't understand for one. So, what does this mean?"

She shrugged, then looked down at her hands, a tiny little fire salamander dancing along her fingertips before disappearing. I marveled at the woman that was my mate. She was powerful, strength personified. And I had no idea who this woman was.

Just the woman I had been with, the woman I craved. The woman that was mine.

But I didn't know her. Just like she didn't know me. That would have to change, because there was no going back from mating. But it felt like we had countless obstacles in our way before we could even get there.

Chase sighed and came forward. "Welcome, Packmate. You're ours. And we protect our own."

Confusion settled in, because things were moving far too fast, but I leaned forward and brushed a kiss along her lips. "Welcome to the Pack."

"Welcome," she whispered as people started going through plans of what we needed to do—about the Pack, the den, the war, everything that came with being leaders in the Pack. I sat there and listened. I knew that our lives had been irrevocably changed. And I would have to find a way to prove to her that this wasn't a mistake. That her protecting me, sacrificing for me, was worth it.

And then I had to make myself believe. Let myself give in.

Because I hadn't wanted a mate. But now I had one.

And there would be no going back. No pretending, no breaking.

Much like the people in this room, our mating had been forced, hadn't been a true choice. Because the moon goddess had changed the game. We would have to change with it.

I wanted to love my mate, to protect her. So I would find a way to do it. Just like I would find a way to protect my den.

And as I ignored the new beast within me, and understood that this was only the beginning, I knew that this was our next phase.

There would never be any going back.

Even as we were in a war that would soon come to an end.

One way or the other.

THIRTEEN

Malphas

Malphas threw his hand out, knocking everything off the mantle. Somebody screamed as glass shattered, but he ignored it.

These damn wolves. His chest heaved and he continued to pace.

"Darling?" Lilith asked from beside him, and he whirled, catching her by the throat. For an instant he saw fear.

Fear he hadn't seen in her before. She had never been scared of him. No, she had always wanted him. Had always devoured him in every way possible.

But now he had scared her. Perhaps, though, it was time.

He let go of her, only to pull her hair then rub his thumb along her jaw.

"The wolves stopped our power."

His voice was a purr, so dangerous that he knew anyone in hearing distance would scatter like the mice they were. Vermin who didn't even deserve to be near him.

"It's the witch. How did the witch know?"

Malphas snarled, and then went back to pacing again, leaving Lilith where she stood.

She didn't move, scared again. That was good. She needed to be scared.

"That power within her. The power that will be ours."

"You want her still?" Lilith asked, and he heard the jealousy. He wanted to dismiss it, but he couldn't yet, not when he needed to understand what was happening. Not when he needed the power to cascade in a way that meant it would be his.

"I want her power. It will be mine." He paused. "And yours."

Her eyes lit up.

"We will rip open her power, find the seed of it, and make it ours. We will siphon it all."

"And we will destroy the Aspens. They hurt you.

They hurt us. And they cannot even stand to fight us again."

"Never. I was going to use them as our cannon fodder, to turn them into our hybrid army, but they only deserve death. We will use the others of the alliance as our hybrids, and they will never know what's coming at them."

Lily gestured towards the balcony, and he nodded. "Let us see what my years of waiting have brought. We lost our generals, the vampires who thought to steal the powers from us."

"This is what you always wanted. The power of the world."

"And we will have it." He slid his finger along her jaw again, and she shivered. "We have our inside man. The one who will change everything. We will stop the Aspens finally."

"And the one who is a traitor to them all?"

"It is time to call him forth. For him to know his true purpose."

Lilith smiled, and he opened the doors to the balcony, taking a step out.

Thousands stood there, under the control of his generals, waiting.

Malphas had spent a decade fine-tuning his venom in

order to create the perfect vampire. And from there, he created his hybrids.

Now, with the cunning mastery of his own power, he held strength that nobody understood.

Cheers began to ring out as they caught sight of him, and Malphas smiled. Lilith stood beside him, his first general at his other side. They flanked him in power, but he was the true strength.

Malphas held up his arm, and the cheering ceased immediately.

"We will destroy the Aspens. We will destroy the wolves. And from there, we will take their corpses and show the world what happens when you rise against us. Previous wolves and demons and monsters thought they could rule, but they did not have the strength nor the cunning to make it happen. But we have been waiting. We have used magic and power that they have only dreamed of. And once they realize who the true seekers are, they will bow before us."

Shouts rang out, as the vampires and hybrids began to chant, "Malphas! Malphas!"

The demon smiled then, his eyes glowing gold.

The bond within his heart that connected him to his brothers on the other side pulsed. They were waiting for their time. They knew Malphas was the strongest one. The one who would hold the line for when they came.

For this was just the first step. Once the Aspens were killed, the other Packs of the alliance would fall. And then they would take over the rest of the nation, and the world, and the demons who had been waiting on the other side would come.

It was time for hell to reign on earth. It was time for the end of the human civilization, for the end of the wolves.

And they would call him master.

For Malphas was the power. The future. And their unending god.

CHAPTER
FOURTEEN

Steele

IN THE FEW WEEKS SINCE THE ATTACK, EVERYTHING had changed.

I still wasn't quite sure what the hell I was supposed to be doing, but there was no going back now. No looking back and wondering how to fix this.

But in the weeks since I had become who I was now, since the new bond within me pulsed, we had somehow found a routine.

Keeping the Pack safe, hunting vampires, and ignoring talks of the future and who we were.

Jade had moved in soon after we had finally been released from the clinic. She had said point-blank it didn't make any sense for her to stay away since there was no going back, and we had been sleeping together anyway.

That had made me smile, something I hadn't expected to do that day, or any day since, and I just shook my head and brought her few belongings back to my place.

She still didn't have enough things, though she never complained.

It killed me that I couldn't provide more for my mate, mostly because she wouldn't let me.

So, although I was still figuring this out, I tried to get her something every day. I wouldn't hand it to her of course. I would just put it in her dresser and she'd find it on her own. A sweater that I figured she might want when it got colder. She wasn't a wolf with excess body heat, but she was a fire witch, so she could probably make her own heat, but I wanted her to have the damn sweater. I'd gotten her an extra pair of boots so she could hike along the trails that wound throughout the den. She hadn't had any. I was going to do my best to provide for her. Even if she didn't want me to.

Hayes was a woodworker, and when I had asked him to make me something for her, he had just raised a brow and made a little songbird with its wings on fire. I had placed it on her nightstand, and she hadn't thrown it away. In fact, I had heard her say thank you to Hayes, then looked at me, eyes narrowed.

Oh, she knew what I was doing. I was trying to take care of my mate. I might not have wanted one, but I had one, and I refused to run away from it.

"Are you just going to stand there and stare at our bed with a frown on your face?"

I looked over my shoulder to see Jade, books in hand and a frown on her face. She had pulled her hair back from her face with a clip, though most of it still fell down her back. There had never been any question that Jade was stunning. I had wanted her from the moment I saw her, hence why I had stayed away. But now there was no going back. No *wanting* to go back.

Maybe that was my fault, but I couldn't change it now. So I might as well figure out what the hell I was doing.

"I'm just thinking about what else you need."

She rolled her eyes and set the stack of books down on the table beside her. "I don't need much. Other than maybe figuring out who the traitor is."

I growled, but it didn't sound like the wolf. Instead it sounded like the other thing, the thing I was trying to figure out. Concern rushed over her face, but she pushed it away.

"I haven't shifted into that form again. Don't know if I

should," I said after a moment. Of all people, she was the one I could trust with this. After all, she had saved my life. There was no purpose in hiding it. In doing that, I'd only hurt her. And I had done that enough. I needed to find a better way to survive.

"If you do, I'd like to be there."

I raised a brow. "Really?"

"Really. I think maybe I'd help? Or I'll make it worse. I'm not quite sure. But either way, I'll be there. We're not going to let that fucking demon win."

My lips twitched into a smile at that, and I nodded. "Damn straight. So yeah, we'll stop it. Because I don't really think we have another choice. Are you meeting with Dara soon?" I asked, not sure how to change the subject. Everything felt so fucking awkward. We'd been thrown into this and had been so busy trying to protect everyone else, we'd skipped all the important steps. I knew I wanted her, and we reached for each other in the night, knowing the physical parts of us were the only things that actually made sense.

But everything else? I didn't know what I was doing.

"Soon. With the coven. We're shoring up the wards, and that means we need to meet often."

"I have a meeting with the lieutenants at four."

"And I guess dinner when we get home?" Jade

frowned before she laughed, shaking her head. "That sounds so domestic. Like a normal day. There's nothing normal about this."

"I was just thinking that we skipped some important parts," I said honestly.

"True, and since there's no severing this, maybe we should deal with that? But that sounds like a lot of work and I'm really tired." She rubbed her temples, and I reached out without thinking, putting my hands above hers. She froze before leaning into my touch. Again, the physical parts we had down. But this seemed more than that. Maybe I needed to give in, or at least trust, not run away.

"You want to go for a walk?"

She raised a brow. "Really? Just the two of us?"

"Unless we see a pup or a cub frolicking, then we can play with them. I know you love playing with the babies."

It had been somewhat of a surprise to see Jade holding Chase and Skye's new infant. She had looked so right and had even made a little ball of fire dance above the baby. She had been safe no matter what, she just liked seeing the lights, but Jade looked for all the world like she was carefree.

"Well, if we see a pup then I'm going to have to play. I'm sorry, but they win. Every time."

"That makes sense." I paused. "Do you want them? Kids?"

Such an awkward conversation for people who were mated on a soul level, but we were still figuring it out.

Jade winced. "You know, the answer was always no. Because I was on the run. Figuring out my own powers. But the answer to mating was also a no before this."

I held out my hand, and she slid her fingers into mine. We began our walk, and I tried to figure out how to do this.

I wasn't good with feelings. With memories. No, I was the asshole who got shit done and protected his Pack. I wasn't supposed to care about more than that.

But I could sense her struggle along our bond. And that meant I needed to do better.

But dammit, I wasn't good at this.

"What do you know of the Pack before Chase was Alpha?" I asked, broaching a subject that I wanted nothing to do with. But Jade had saved my life, had tied herself to me even though she didn't want to, so she deserved my truth.

Jade pressed her lips together and sighed. "I know about Blade. As I told Cole when he figured out his past, I met Blade."

I nodded, remembering now. "Blade tried to force you

into the Pack." It wasn't a question, but she answered anyway.

"Yes. He wanted my power. And as you know now, I have extra fire within me. It's not of the demon, it's not of death, but it is something that can be used against others in a way to gain more power. Blade wanted it. And I knew I couldn't give that to him."

"The firebird—is it hereditary?"

She shook her head. "No. Although my family are all fire witches and had more flame than others. Elemental witches are able to call only elements. And I can do that, I do do that, but there's something else inside me. Like a phoenix rising from the ashes. Every time I use more fire, it builds up, and then I have this extra pull. That's why I'm able to calm what's inside you along our mating bond. Because of the extra."

I nodded as we turned the corner, walking deeper into the forest. "So the more you use your magic, the calmer I'll be?" I asked, somewhat joking.

"I don't think I could calm you completely. I wouldn't want to. I like you in your asshole mode."

"You're just as much of an asshole as me," I teased.

She rolled her eyes, her lips splitting into a grin. "Damn straight. We just get things done."

"I'd ask you if you just called me a bitch, but I did just call you an asshole. I deserve that."

"Yes, you are my bitch," she teased, and I squeezed her hand, laughing when I didn't think I would when it came to this conversation.

"My parents were amazing. Strong taskmasters, but they protected me. And when Blade sent his men, they tried to save me." She paused, and I could feel the pain along the bond. I wanted to fix it, to soothe her, but I knew she needed that pain. Just like I needed mine. One can't survive without their past, to be that phoenix out of those ashes. So I just stood there and listened as she explained.

"They died, and I hated myself for it for a while. And when I couldn't figure out how to control the fire within me, I met Sawyer." I raised a brow, and she smiled. "Sawyer and I have never slept together. We're just friends who lean on each other during the worst times. I don't want to tell all of his story, but he was on the run for his own reasons. And when we found ourselves fighting a rival coven who wanted our powers, ones just as dark as the coven that Malphas murdered, Sawyer and I saved each other. And Declan and the others. Dara as well. We all leaned on each other, though we had to be secret about it. Had to hide from other covens. And so we split up, but Sawyer stayed with me. We just clicked. He's like my pesky brother."

I laughed. "He is pesky."

"And I've never had feelings for him like that. I can promise you."

"Well, you're my mate now. I guess I should get over my jealousy."

"Yes, let's just tell a dominant wolf newly mated with mating urges that jealousy shouldn't be an issue. I'll stand here and wait while you figure that out."

I stopped then shook my head. Then I brushed her hair back from her face and smiled.

"Sarcasm. I like it."

"It's my love language." She paused, winced. "Or just my language."

Again, it was this weird thing. Mates were supposed to be in love. We were potentially the other halves of each other's soul, and we could feel one another along that bond. But we didn't love each other yet. I thought maybe my wolf would one day. But I had never expected this. We were doing it all backwards, and I didn't want to hurt her along the way. Because I knew hell was coming, a war that would break us, and she didn't deserve to have me break her.

"While Blade was searching for you and others to create his dark magic Pack, he was using the witches he had and his dominance to break us from within."

Her smile fell as I began, and she brushed her fingers along my jaw. My wolf leaned into her, as did the beast, and I let out a breath, knowing I needed to tell her even though I didn't want to.

"Blade forced us to do what he wanted. He forced us to change who we were. He would order me using his dominance, so my wolf couldn't disobey. He used dark magic in order to enhance that dominance. Chase is far more dominant than his father ever was, but because Blade was able to use dark magic to enhance that, Chase couldn't fight back. Audrey nearly died fighting to get help."

I shook my head. "But when I was younger, I couldn't do anything. My parents tried. And that's what killed them."

"Steele, you don't have to tell me."

"No." She'd figure out why I was so hesitant to touch anything with the future, anything with a connection. "It's why I didn't want to mate. At least I hadn't," I added quickly. But she didn't look hurt. She looked understanding. Again, she hadn't wanted to mate either. I understood where she came from, so now it was my turn. "They held me down with chains and magic. And they whipped me in front of my parents."

"The scars on your back," she whispered.

I nodded jerkily. "They beat me, rubbed magic salt into the wounds so they would scar. All to punish my parents for trying to save an elder wolf who hadn't wanted to live under Blade's rule. And when my parents got to be too much, when the wolves in charge needed to punish *me*, they decapitated my parents in front of me. Blood sprayed, covering my face, and I screamed, my wolf howled. But it wasn't enough. My parents died in front of me, died for each other, and I had to watch. I was sixteen, and my wolf nearly broke then. I thought I was going insane, and it took the dominance of my Alpha forcing me to do his bidding, that saved me." I laughed ironically, hating myself.

"If he hadn't wanted me to survive in order to use my strength, I'd have died right then. Because I was bonded to my parents too. When that bond snapped, it broke me. And that's why I hadn't wanted to add a new bond. Even when the moon goddess got it into her head that I needed one, not only did she allow this mating, but she made me an Enforcer. So it's my job to protect our Pack. I'm bonded to them in a way that others aren't, and this demon is damaging that. He's tainting it. So I'm trying to figure this out. And figure us out with you."

Tears streaked down her face as she cupped my cheeks.

"Steele. I'm so sorry. So damn sorry."

I shook my head, knowing there wasn't much more to say.

"We didn't ask for this. But we're here. And I can feel

you. Along the bond. I feel like we could have more. But I'm freaking the fuck out, Jade."

I hadn't meant to say that part, hadn't meant to be so honest, but there was no more time for lies or shields. Not when I knew something was coming. Something we would need each other for, more than we'd ever thought possible.

"I have all this power and I don't know what to do with it," she whispered. "And you're right, we didn't ask for this. But there is no going back. So we go our own way, backwards and twisted. But I trust you, Steele. And I never thought I would say those words to anyone else."

Relieved, my wolf nuzzled into me, wanting her, needing her touch. So I leaned down and took her lips with mine. Just a small kiss, just a thank you.

We stood on the edge of the clearing, alone for now, between patrols. I held onto my mate, wondering how the hell we had gotten here.

"So we figure out this Pack, protect our people, and then we figure out each other."

She laughed then and rolled her eyes. "Yes. That makes fucking sense. We'll just put it on a list. A little to-do list for things we need to do. Protect the Pack, find the traitor, kill a demon, oh, and get to know my mate. Got it."

"Well, it's either a list or we sit in the corner and never talk to each other."

"Well, I guess we'll figure this out. Because I don't want to hurt you. I know this isn't what you wanted."

I held back a wince at that, but I nodded tightly. "And I know I'm not who you wanted. But we made our choices. And we won't go back."

"Because of duty," she said, her voice slightly hollow.

I didn't know what more she wanted, what I should say.

"Duty has brought me this far. I don't think it can go on."

Something went past her eyes, and maybe she wanted me to say I loved her. But that would be a lie. Wouldn't it? I wanted her. I craved her. I liked her, but I didn't know her. And this had been forced upon us. This wasn't our choice. So I needed time. Even if she hated me.

The hairs on the back of my neck stood on end as I tried to think of what to say, and I turned, wondering what the hell was going on in the wards behind us.

"Oh my God," she whispered.

I put myself in front of Jade, not thinking, as I saw the man in front of us, the man at the wards.

But I had to be seeing things. This couldn't be true.

Of all people, it couldn't have been him.

But Cassius stood at the wards, his eyes glassy as he smiled and cut into his palms.

"*I am of the master,*" Cassius said, his voice deep, low,

devoid of emotion. *"And you will fall to his power. And you will see his light. His glory. And you will surrender."*

When Cassius cut again I ran towards him. Jade was behind me, fire burning, and then Cassius smiled and the world exploded.

CHAPTER
FIFTEEN

Steele

WE WERE THRUST THROUGH THE WARDS AND MY BODY slammed to the ground. Whatever explosion had just happened was still ringing in my ears.

Shoulder aching, I rolled to my feet as I searched for Jade amongst the fire and smoke, and I nearly roared at the sight of her.

She lay on the ground, struggling to get up as I moved towards her. She looked up at me, a gash on her forehead and fire in her eyes. "Steele! Behind you."

I ducked and turned, claws outstretched as I dug into the first vampire. It fell before me, neck gaping open from where I had sliced through its flesh, but that wasn't the only thing I was watching.

"Dear goddess," I whispered, my hands shaking.

It didn't make any sense. But it had to be. This had to be it. Jade was at my side in an instant, fire licking up her arms. Off in the distance, an army marched. An army of darkness bound for the den.

And we were in their line of fire.

We were their battle.

We wouldn't be enough if we didn't move fast. I quickly alerted the others through my alarm, but I was so damn afraid I'd be too late.

"Malphas brought them all. The *bastard* brought them all."

Jade coughed beside me. "He's been waiting for this moment."

I turned, realization finally hitting me as I saw Cassius kneeling on the ground, hands over his head as he rocked back and forth. Blood streamed down his hands and arms. It didn't make any sense.

This couldn't be true.

But then again, it had to be.

Cassius was the traitor. Maybe unwilling, maybe not realizing what he had been doing this whole time. But my friend, the man who had stood by my side for years, who had helped piece me back together when my parents died, who had lovingly and achingly claimed his mate during a time where our former Alpha hadn't allowed us to find mates. Cassius was the traitor.

And there'd be no coming back from it.

My friend looked up at me with blood-filled eyes and shook his head. "What happened? What happened?"

Rage filled me, thinking about every single person who had been hurt, who had *died* because of this man. Because of what the demon had done to him.

I couldn't think, I couldn't focus.

Before I could figure out what to do, what to say to the man who had been my friend but who had threatened us all, everything seemed to happen at once.

Another bomb went off on the other side of the den, rattling the bonds within me. The vampires that had come with that first attack began moving closer. But they weren't alone.

The Human Union, or whatever the fuck they were calling themselves these days, were with them.

It appeared that the human organization figured they could work with the vampires and demon to get what they wanted. They just wanted us shifters out of the way. Magic users that they couldn't control.

With the way the territory was situated, we were the southernmost Pack in our alliance. We were mostly surrounded by trees, with the Pacific coast to our west, but there was also a huge field to the north of us, a clearing where we used to host Pack meetings and other events. But right now it was our battlefield. One where they would stop at nothing to get to us.

Gavin was at my side in an instant, eyes wide. "What the hell?"

"It was Cassius. Cassius is our traitor." The words were ripped out of me, torn from my throat as my wolf and the beast inside raged at the betrayal. The three souls within my body finally coming together in one emotion: agony.

My former friend looked up at me, blood on his face, and shook his head. "I didn't know. He didn't tell me. *What was coming.* I didn't know what was happening. How is this happening?" he continued to mumble, rubbing his hands over his face.

I moved forward and gripped Cassius by his neck. I didn't know if this was the true Cassius, or what Malphas created, and that meant I couldn't trust him. I couldn't lean into the friendship that had lasted decades. I had to protect my mate and my Pack...and then I could protect my friend. Whatever was left of him. "What else did you give them, Cassius? What happened?"

"I didn't know I was doing it. Kill me, Steele. I don't know what else I can do. Just end this. Let me protect them. Let me do the one thing I should have been doing all this time."

My wolf howled and the beast within me rumbled.

Because *that* was the Cassius I knew. The man who would sacrifice himself to protect his den. Someone had hurt him, had taken from him, and I was too angry to see past that.

"Keep him still, watch him," I ordered my two lieutenants when they came forward. "I don't know what else the demon wants him to do, but if Cassius didn't do this on his own, then we're going to fix this."

I was the Enforcer, not the Alpha, so it was Chase who would have the final word. But that didn't mean anything, not now.

I turned to see Jade standing, her back to me with her hands out, whispering magical spells in order to put another shield between the den and the oncoming force.

We only had minutes, if that, to formulate a plan, because though we had been preparing for this, we hadn't been prepared for the wards to fail.

And in the explosion, I hadn't realized the true scope of the horror involved.

Because our wards that had bonded us together were down.

There was no stopping the force from coming and hurting our innocent. From wiping out our den.

This was the final battle. And if we didn't stop it, there would be no survivors.

"What else can I do?" Declan asked, and I whirled to see the witch coming towards me, as well as the rest of the coven who had been on the den property to meet with Jade later.

"Help me set up new wards. They won't be strong enough to stop them, but we can slow them down."

Declan nodded, then went to Jade's side. He held up his hands and began whispering curses at the same time, as did the other coven members, hands outstretched, forming a magical wall as the humans and vampires stood at the other end of the clearing. Waiting.

I didn't know what they were waiting for. For Cassius to do something else? For us to realize there was no hope?

Or for us to make the first move?

All I knew was we had these moments to regroup, to set our stage.

And if we weren't careful, this would be the last.

"Cassius?" a soft voice asked from the side as everyone ran around, doing what they were told. Pack members went to their assigned areas, ready to fight, ready to protect the pups. I knew, because we had trained for this, the other Packs were being contacted. The Redwoods, Talons, and Centrals would be protecting their own dens and would be sending us people to help us win this battle.

The demon was here, I could feel it as the hybrid within me pushed, wanting out.

If this was the final battle, we would make it through. We would change everything.

But, in that moment, I could only look at the woman running towards us, face ashen.

Novah, Cassius's mate, and a Truth Seeker.

When her powers were invoked, she could sense the truth from anyone. She could see if someone was lying. She could sense their deceptions.

But she hadn't sensed her mate's deception.

As the lieutenants held Cassius back, I moved towards Novah, arm outstretched.

"That's far enough," I snarled.

She stopped, eyes wide, hands outstretched. Novah, while a Truth Seeker, was also a latent wolf. She couldn't shift into her wolf form, though she could use her claws in human form in order to fight.

She was a soldier, one I trusted. One I should have been able to trust.

"Did you know? Did you know that Cassius was the one betraying us?" I snapped.

Tears fell down Novah's face as she shook her head, palms up.

"Let me deal with this," Audrey said softly as she moved forward. "I'm the Beta, this is my problem."

"It's all of our problem if she knew."

"I didn't know," Novah cried out. "How did I not know that my mate was the traitor?"

"I'm sorry," Cassius whispered, blood still dripping from his eyes. "I didn't either. How many others have been hurt by this demon because we didn't understand his magic? Because we weren't strong enough?"

The demons and those particular humans wanted to wipe out the shifters. And they were winning.

What else were we missing?

"What did the demon do to him?" Novah asked as Audrey moved forward and cupped her face. I didn't know what was said, because Chase growled, and I had to look towards my Alpha.

"This is it. We're done being on the defensive."

I nodded tightly. "Pack is life."

Chase looked at all of us, his wolf in his eyes, the gold gaze dominating and furious, but not angry *at* us. No, the rage was for the demon and everything that had happened in these past few years, culminating in this moment.

"Long live the Pack! Long live the Aspens!" Chase bellowed, and I howled, throwing my head back in agreement. I looked towards Jade, who had her hands out, flames pouring from her palms.

"They're coming. I don't know how much longer I can

hold this. It's enough for now, but it's not as secure as the full wards."

I ran towards her and nodded. "We've got this. Stand by my side?"

She looked at me, then back at Cassius and Novah, who looked as if their whole world had broken, and in reality, it had. "Okay. Okay."

I gripped her chin and kissed her hard, needing her taste.

There wasn't anything for me to say, I didn't have the words. Because this was what we had been fighting towards. The demon had never come out like this, had never come directly at us. And that meant we had to fight.

And I didn't want to tell her that we would be fine, that we would come out of this alive. As it was, whatever the hell was inside me, this hybrid I was trying to soothe, told me that we were far closer to our ending than I'd ever thought possible.

But she gripped my hip and nodded tightly as the world exploded again.

We moved as one, doing what we had all trained for, and I knew if we didn't stop this now, there'd be no hope for our future. The demon wanted us, wanted our ending. And I'd be damned if we allowed that to happen.

Scores of vampires, hybrids, and humans ran at us,

hatred on their faces, fangs bared, claws out, and humans with their weapons.

But we were the Aspens, and we were fighting with everything we had.

I knew the other Packs would be here soon, and we would have to hold the line until they got here. Because there were thousands of vampires. I never thought there could be that many. But the demon had been given decades to plan for and build to this moment.

But we would not fail.

I thought of the small pups who were now going to their evacuation points with the maternals and submissives as their protectors. No, we would make sure they had their future. Because we hadn't had a future before. Not with Blade. But with Chase, and the other Alphas, we would have this.

There was no other choice.

We moved through the new wards, as they were meant to protect the weaker and defenseless members of our Pack. I knew from my earpiece that we weren't completely surrounded yet, and the forces seemed to be concentrated on this side of the former wards. I had members all around the den waiting for an ambush on the other side in case this was a distraction, but the new wards that the witches had put up so quickly would at least give the other members a chance to retreat and hide and protect themselves. They wouldn't last for long. But it had to be something.

Jade was at my side, Cruz on the other, as the first wave of vampires came.

I let the wolf come forward, knowing I could shift faster than most because of the moon goddess's new ways. It no longer took fifteen minutes of brutal shifting and changing, instead it could be in an instant, the pain still just as intense, just consolidated. For now, though, I used claws and fangs to get through the first wave of vampires.

Audrey and Gavin were on one end of the field, fighting with Ronan and a few other soldiers. We had to get through these humans and vampires and hybrids in order to get to the demon and his consort. Once they were dealt with, we could get through the rest. But if we didn't take out the demon, he would continue to make more and more vampires, and more and more of those who wanted to kill us.

So we had to take him out. I just didn't know who was strong enough to do so. Perhaps our Alpha. But I'd be damned if I'd let him die for us.

Audrey rolled to the ground, her claws out as she took out one vampire, then the next. When three humans came forward, guns ready, Gavin moved so fast he was a blur. Then he shifted into his wolf form and tore out the throats of the humans who threatened to shoot his mate.

Chase and Skye were on the other end, my Alpha moving with such ferocity that some vampires turned and ran. I didn't know if their master, the one controlling them, was doing it, or if perhaps they had the sense to run from an Alpha who could kill them in just one movement.

Skye was there, not a submissive, not a dominant. She was the one to soothe the broken Alpha as the Gamma. And she could fight like nobody else. She was quick and agile, leaping on the nearest vampire, taking him out, then going to the next.

The fact that their child was back with the Redwoods, safe behind their wards, I knew was too much for them. But we were all fighting, knowing that if we didn't stop this now, there'd be no end to this pain. Out of the corner of my eye I saw Cole and Nico come forward, Adalyn with them. Good, the Centrals were here now. Their Heir and Beta were here too, fighting amongst the huge horde of vampires and humans and hybrids.

The three of them pushed through the horde, an odd sense of magical mayhem sliding through them. I knew that was the triad bond, something I had only seen in action once, but here they were, fighting with all that they had to protect all of us. To protect their child.

Cruz and Dara were near me, Dara killing each vampire with a single blow using her death magic to wipe them out. She took down a hybrid, along with Cruz, and screamed as black magic sliced out of her and deep into the hybrid in front of her.

The hybrid died, a quick death, and that was the only good that came out of it.

I knew that the hybrid had had no choice. If Jade hadn't been there for me, if she hadn't sacrificed part of her future and mated with me in order to save me, I would be right there with them. A hybrid with no sense of self, fighting at my master's bidding.

And dying, because there was no way to save me.

Sawyer was a few feet in front of Jade, slicing through vampires as he moved. He was quick, efficient, and he wasn't alone. Wynter was there, slicing through them, Blake beside them. He had his claws out, but was also using his blades, taking out as many as they could.

Wren went from Pack member to Pack member, healing who she could. Because we were all getting injured, all trying to duck out of the way of bite marks. For those who were unlucky to be bitten, and then frozen in whatever pain that the vampires gave us, she used her healing and the new poultice to stop whatever rampaged through us as we got hurt. The witches and Healers together had come up with this, and here we were, finally putting their combined efforts into good use.

As I turned around, taking out a vampire who had snuck up behind us, I saw Cassius fighting alongside

Novah. It seemed that some of the vampires had broken through the ranks and my lieutenants had been needed. But now the traitor was fighting for us. And that broke me. Because I knew that Cassius hadn't done it on purpose. That he had been a vessel, like I had been when I was forced to become a hybrid.

It wasn't his fault, and yet he had been marked in flames just like the rest of us.

"You think you can stop me?" Malphas called from the other end of the field. His voice echoed throughout, as if there was a magical means enhancing it. He wasn't even fighting. No, he stood there, a smile on his evil face, as his consort stood beside him—Lily, with her bright eyes and cruel smile.

There was something wrong with her though, her hand shooks and she was covered in sweat.

If I didn't know better, I would say that she was going through withdrawal. And maybe she was. Jade had said she was a siphon, a magical user.

An abuser.

And now she wanted more magic. But the only magic users on this field were the coven and my mate. So fuck that. I wouldn't allow them to be siphoned.

"You are nothing. We will fight everything to stop you," I growled out.

"And it won't be enough. You animals have never been enough."

Malphas flicked his hand, and another wave of vampires rushed out of the tree line, this time with fire in their palms.

Jade screamed, "Demon fire! He gave them demon fire."

I frowned. "What?"

"It's the opposite of my power in how it's created and birthed. I can call forth the demon flame and turn into a firebird. That is how I can control the hybrid and how I have so much extra fire, but he somehow gave something similar to these vampires. I don't know how, but we have to stop them. If we don't, they'll burn down this entire forest and I won't be able to stop it."

I cursed under my breath and moved towards them, Jade at my side. Cruz and Dara followed close behind, as if sensing we were going to need help. And I knew we would.

But then I screamed out a too-late warning.

Ronan stood in front of Audrey, who was kneeling on the ground, a bloody gash on her shoulder so deep I could see bone.

"Run!" she called out, but the young wolf didn't. Instead he stood in front of a vampire with flame in his palms, and clawed out. The vampire fell, neck gaping open, but Ronan wasn't fast enough.

Ronan shouted as flame engulfed him, and the new wolf, the one who had protected us all and then learned how to control his wolf, fell to his knees, screaming in pain.

Audrey stood up, arm limp at her side, as she clawed through another vampire, dodging the flame. She went to Ronan, trying to protect him, and we ran.

But we weren't fast enough.

Ronan ley out one last scream, and then fell, body still on fire, and the world felt like it was ending.

"No!" Audrey, his trainer and friend, screamed.

She had been his trainer, as had I, and I'd be damned if we'd lose anyone else.

The bond between us snapped, and I knew Ronan was gone. The bonds as Enforcer no longer needed to keep him safe, because I had already failed. The young wolf who had protected so many with his charm and strength was gone.

Jade called out and slammed more fire into the vampires. They let out piercing screams, the remaining seven of them with flames going to their knees as they burned to a crisp. The wings on Jade's back fluttered before they disappeared, and she pushed more magic towards them.

"I was too late. Damn it, I was too late for him."

"We need to stop the demon, no matter what," I said as I gripped her shoulders, trying to keep us both together.

She nodded tightly, and then let out another shout.

Malphas moved so quickly I could barely see him. But suddenly he was in front of Chase.

My wolf roared and I lunged forward, shifting into wolf form in an instant.

I was faster as a wolf, and I needed to get to my Alpha. My paws slammed the ground as I ran towards Chase.

Malphas took Skye by the neck and threw her across the field. She thudded to the ground, limp and unmoving.

Chase howled, raking his claws down the demon's flank. The demon just smiled and held out his palm, magic spewed in a rush from him.

I was going to be too late.

The demon was far too powerful, and he was going to kill my Alpha.

But I had to go, I had to save him.

I kept moving, putting all of myself into it, but then another moved faster.

As Malphas thrust his hand out in what should be the killing blow for our Alpha, Cassius moved in front of him.

He threw his body in front of Chase and roared.

Magic pulsed, and the demon flew back, as if ricocheting off his own magic that he had put into Cassius.

The demon rolled, and Lily ran to his side. Out of the corner of my eye I saw Wren running to Skye, but she kept looking towards us, and I shook my head.

Because what lay in front of me I knew couldn't be saved, though Skye could.

It wasn't a choice I wanted to make, but it wasn't a choice at all.

We didn't have time, others were still fighting, even as what had just transpired started to wash over us.

But Chase looked at me, and then knelt down and held Cassius close to him.

"I tried to fight it," Cassius whispered, blood pooling from him.

Chase nodded, and I knelt beside him, Jade at my side.

"You saved me. You're a good wolf, a good man," Chase said, voice softer and kinder than a battlefield warranted.

Cassius blinked and sucked in a breath. "I guess that's why the moon goddess has never blessed me. Because she knew this would happen. That I would be the weak link."

I shook my head, fangs bared. "You were always the strongest. You were always there for me. For all of us. This is the demon. It wasn't you."

"But I saved you, in the end," he whispered before his

chest stopped moving. Chase sat there, hands shaking. I didn't have any words, I couldn't say anything.

Behind me I heard Novah scream, the mating bond breaking between her and Cassius. Somehow it had survived a spell that had forced Cassius to betray us all. But now it was gone, and as Skye lay limp, but alive, in the Healer's hands, I knew that if we didn't end this soon, I would lose more friends than I already had. Each passing moment increased the chance that I would lose everything.

I looked at Jade, who nodded.

"I know what you have to do," she said, and I took a deep breath.

I would have to use my hybrid and pray to the goddess that I could control it with Jade's help.

Because this was the only thing I had that was strong enough in my arsenal to take out the demon.

Only I didn't know if it would be enough.

And I had a feeling that I might just lose everything before this battle ended. Including myself.

SIXTEEN

Jade

Power slammed into me as another wave of magic filled the air. It wasn't done by the demon, no, this was from my fellow witches.

Declan ran towards us, blood on his hands, but he didn't look hurt.

He just shook off whatever pain was hitting him and came forward with Bishop and Dara by his side. "What can we do?" he asked.

The fire within me burned and I knew if I didn't release it soon, I'd burn from within. I knew exactly who I wanted to reach out towards. Exactly who needed this fire.

"Settle the wards, anchor them. And go find Wren. She's dealing with wounds from the hybrids and vampires that she can't handle on her own. Perhaps with the coven she'll be strengthened."

Declan looked at me, then out at the battlefield as people fought on. "Are you sure? We can go on the offensive."

Leah, a woman with kind eyes, moved forward and put her hand on his arm. "We will heal. We are the base, the ones who protect. Go, Jade. Do what you have to. We'll be waiting."

Bishop didn't say anything, his eyes filled with pain. But with his magic it made sense.

The other members of the coven, those connected to the Talons and Redwoods, were here too, but they were fighting alongside their Packs. If needed, I would pull them in to help the Healers, but they knew what they were doing. They had more years than I did when it came to fighting to protect us.

"We need to stop the demon," Chase said, Skye by his side.

She was pale, her body nearly gray as she glared over at the fighting.

"Should you be here? You should be resting," I said to the Alpha's mate.

Her wolf went into her gaze, and she snarled, "I'm fine."

"She refuses to go back to the den. She'll be sticking close to my side," Chase snapped.

"I watched you almost die, too. So no, I will not be leaving your side."

The two didn't argue any more, they looked between us, and Chase let out a sigh. "Do you hear her?" Chase asked, and I frowned, staring between them.

"Hear who?"

But my mate rubbed over his heart as he nodded. "The moon goddess. She can barely scream over the sound of the demon in our heads, but I know what she wants. And I think I'll be strong enough to do it."

I knew why everything had gone this way.

Why I was here at his side with my special power.

"I can contain the flame of the demon, but I can't take him out."

"But with the strength that he gave me accidentally, I can. But first, we'll have to take care of the poisoner."

"Do it," Wynter said, surprising me. I turned to the human, blood splattered all over her face, and I shook my head.

"Are you okay?"

Wynter nodded. "I'm fine. I might be human, but I'm strong. And I'm not fighting alone. But that monster over there? The one who siphons? She's going to stand in front of her consort to protect him, so take her out. She's not the friend that I had. Lily's long gone. So take out that bitch before I do."

I had never heard Wynter speak like that, but she had been best friends with Lily. The two of them against the world. I hadn't truly thought about the pain that she must have been in at the betrayal. But I had been betrayed too, and I understood it. So I nodded.

"Make a distraction?" I asked, and Chase nodded. "You have all of us. We'll do that. Take out the demon, take out Lily. And let's fucking end this."

Steele looked at me and rolled his shoulders back. "Can you fight Lily and still keep the hybrid at bay?" he asked.

I wasn't sure I knew the answer, but I needed to. So I nodded. "Yes. I can."

And I hoped like hell it wasn't a lie.

There was no time for waiting, no time for resting and healing. If we didn't end this now, the demon would end it for us. It was evident that he was far stronger than us, but unless we used whatever special powers we had, the ones we had been trained for or had thrust upon us, we would die here. All of us would.

The Redwoods fought with a blaze that I had never truly understood before. They were an amalgamation of witches, humans, and shifters. There was even some magic that I had never seen before, but they fought as one, generations fighting together. Mother and daughter, father and son, parent and child. They fought as if they had faced death before, and they had. They had faced demons before and won. And had nearly lost everything in order to make that happen.

On the other side of the field the Talons fought through the hybrids. Each of them had their own special presence, ones that spoke of loss and torment. They fought with the glory that came from the moon goddess's blessings. My friends fought alongside them, ones that had become Talons over the years. They used their magic as witches and humans and shifters, and they barreled through the horror that was this battle.

On the northern side of the clearing, the Centrals battled. Small and compact, the Pack was still growing, but they were fierce. The triad mating bond of the Alpha moved forward, slamming into vampires and stopping them with a single blow. I didn't know how long the triad bond would work, how much energy they had, but they were moving forward, slicing through vampires that seemed to have more magic than usual. The humans fighting alongside the vampires kept moving forward, but some were retreating. They seemed to realize that their human alliance wasn't enough. That they were on the wrong side of history, or perhaps they were more scared of what was fighting alongside them than the hate in their hearts. But either way, even with their guns and knives and weapons, they weren't strong enough for us.

Novah ran through the vampires, as if she didn't care if she died or lost it all—and perhaps she didn't. Her mate was gone. Sacrificed himself to save his Alpha. Perhaps he had been gone long before this, but there was no stopping it, no changing it. She'd already lost it all in her world. She would fight for our people. The pain of having nothing left, of having your world changed forever, meant fighting was inevitable.

Blake fought alongside his parents with the Redwoods, even though death had taken him before, he was fighting amongst all of us. Wynter fought alongside him, her glare on Lily, furious at the betrayal that had taken us all by surprise.

Steele and I fought forward, slicing our way through the vampires and hybrids to get to the demon. Malphas and Lily had retreated to the center and were throwing their worst at us. But we had to get to them. If we didn't stop this, we would die. There was no other option.

Sawyer kept moving, slicing through one vampire then another. But before I could help him, before I could beg him to stay back and stay safe, a vampire moved forward and slammed him to the ground. I screamed, threatened to reach out, but Hayes was there, the big polar bear picking him up, and carrying him to the Healer.

Sawyer was awake, fighting and bleeding. He had to be okay.

It appeared as if there was a cut from a blade on his arm, but that seemed to be it. He had to be okay.

I refused to let my best friend die, but if we didn't keep moving forward, we would all die.

Dara floated over the ground, her toes barely brushing against the dirt as she pushed death magic towards the hybrids and humans threatening them. Cruz cut and killed anyone that came near her. I had never seen my friend accept her death magic as quickly as she had, as deeply. She was a harvester, one who others feared. But she was truth. Because as you lived through the life you were given, death was always on the other side. And she was there to protect against those who brought death too quickly.

Chase and Skye continued to fight, though I knew they were lagging, both of them taking on the mantle of Alpha. Because with each loss, each blow, they felt it along their bonds, and their wolves would stop at nothing to protect their Pack. So if we didn't move fast enough, our Alphas would take everything on themselves. I refused to let that happen.

I ducked out of the way of a firebomb, as Steele shifted to wolf and then back into human. I had never seen anyone shift as quickly while still continuing to move as if he had enough energy to do that forever.

Maybe it was the combination of hybrid and wolf, or maybe it was just how strong my mate was. And how angry.

Audrey and Gavin were off to the side, picking up the bodies of the fallen. I didn't want to count how many we had lost. I wasn't sure I could handle it right then.

But we continued to move.

And suddenly we were there. Lily smiled.

She had been beautiful, once. Innocent in a way that I hadn't realized had been a facade until it was too late.

And now she shook with the power she stole. How many witches had she killed and stolen magic from over the years in order to become the monster she was?

"I can't wait to taste your power. My love has said it would be mine and he has never lied to me."

"You're a monster," I snapped.

"And you are a whore who never understood that my consort wanted you. He wanted you for your power, and you threw it in his face. You didn't understand who you could be with us, and now your power will be mine. Finally."

"Really? You think you can take me with your stolen power? You're not even strong enough to save yourself. You need to lean on a demon that you're fucking in order to be powerful. You are nothing. Not even human. You're just what was below my shoe."

"Bitch!"

Steele gave me a look, as if wondering why the hell I was provoking this bitch, but I needed her away from the demon. We needed to take her out first, and then we could focus our efforts on him.

"Are you ready?" I asked, and he nodded at me. "I trust you," he whispered.

And with that, I knew I loved him. Right then and there, in the most inconvenient time, I loved him. I hadn't meant to fall, and I knew I shouldn't, but he was my mate. Even though fate had destined us, I hadn't let myself trust it.

But this wolf, this dominant wolf who would do anything for his Pack, was giving himself to me. And in that strength, that sense of self, I knew he was mine. I loved him.

I would deal with that later.

I pushed power along the bond and he grinned, knowing exactly what to do.

In an instant he shifted to his hybrid form—seven feet tall, broad, muscled, part wolf, part human, all claws.

I smiled that Lily looked taken aback. Had she not remembered what they had done? Had she not realized that my mate understood exactly how to do this?

I let my own power roll over me, and the wings of my firebird slid out of my back, pounding with their strength.

Lily came at me, magic at her fingertips. She pushed, slamming power into me, but I brushed it off, one swipe after another. She kept going, throwing water, then air, then earth. Every single stolen power she had, but they weren't enough. For I *was* power. I was what she wanted to be. But I had not stolen mine. I had grown into it. This was my birthright. My power. Lily and this demon would not have it.

"I will have yours. And I will feast upon your bones and take everything."

I shuddered at that, knowing she had crossed into bone magic. There were many reasons she could never come back from what she had become, but she was taking yet another step into depravity. I ignored it, knowing if I took a moment to reflect, it would be too much. So I pushed, fire at my fingertips.

"You will never hurt another witch again," I called out.

Lily slammed more magic into me, and I held back my tears and screamed.

I pushed the fire forward, knowing that this might not be enough, but it needed to be. And then the most magical thing I could think of hit me. The bonds of coven grew, we connected to our souls, and suddenly we were enough. The firebird was the focal point, the source, but not all.

Dara's death magic wove into me, intensifying the heat. Gia's fire tangled into mine, Leah's water added intensity, Nico's earth grounded us, Hannah's earth intensified, and Danni, her spirit magic, one I had never touched before, rolled around us, making us stronger.

Declan's metal magic intensified our heat, while Bishop's mental magic made us stronger and focused our power towards Lily. Then Leta, the blood witch, who used blood as protection, always using her own as a sacrifice, wrapped around us all of her knowledge and age, and I knew we were enough.

We were the coven, we were Pack, and we were what Lily always wanted to be.

When Steele put his hand on my shoulder and connected our bond physically and mentally, I knew he was our pillar. The magic of three souls in one, connected to me, was enough.

I smiled.

Lily seemed to know what was happening and

screamed, but there wasn't anything she could do to stop us anymore.

The firebird herself pushed out of my chest and flew towards Lily. The demon looked towards his consort, eyes wide in surprise, and I knew I would carry that memory to my grave.

It was the look of the demon losing someone he hadn't realized he wanted to keep. Lily screamed, and then there was nothing, just the magic she had siphoned and stolen spilling back into the air. Tears burned my eyes.

We weren't done, not nearly.

Because Malphas was still there, standing over the ashes of the woman that had been his, growling.

"You think you are strong enough to take me? I am of the demon realm. And you are nothing."

"And I can call forth your flame," I shouted over all of the elements pounding into us. We had done some magic that I had never heard of before, and this wasn't the end, but we needed to stop him.

When Malphas moved forward, claws outstretched, Steele in his hybrid form stepped in front of me and slammed his hands into Malphas' chest.

Malphas took a step back, I think surprising all of us. Because Steele shouldn't be that strong, but he was connected to us. All Packs, all magics. He was the vessel, and I was the source, and we would take out this demon.

Steele punched out, slamming his fist into Malphas' jaw, and Malphas hit back, landing a blow on Steele in the ribs.

They slashed into each other, blood seeping down Steele's side as claws dug in, but he kept going, slam after slam, punch after punch.

And then Chase was there, and Cruz. All of the Talons and Aspens and Redwoods and Centrals were there, taking Malphas out step by step, hit by hit. Vampires kept trying to get in the way but we took care of them, the same with the hybrids, and the demon kept coming, kept hitting.

But Steele was always in the center, always strong enough. He had to be.

Malphas moved forward again, one eye missing, blood pooling from his mouth, and grabbed Steele by the throat. I screamed, pushing out more magic.

Malphas flicked me away as if I was nothing. I slammed to the ground, spending more time than normal trying to get up, and staggering when I finally made it to my feet.

He shook Steele and grinned, and I knew this was the end. I would die right along with my mate. I would never be able to tell him that I loved him.

This couldn't be the end. It couldn't. And then something happened that I couldn't quite understand.

A split in the air, as if someone had taken a knife to reality itself and sliced it open behind Malphas. The demon dropped Steele, my mate landing on all fours, and looking up at the demon.

"No. No!" the demon called out.

Steele just grinned before he reached out and took my hand.

Steele was so warm, his body shaking and covered in blood, but he was strong.

He had to be.

"You'll pay for this. You'll die," Malphas screeched.

"Not before you," Steele said so quietly that it felt as if it were barely a whisper.

And then Steele punched out, slamming his fist into Malphas' chest.

The demon staggered back, hitting the edges of the opening in time and space, and I understood what had just happened.

Because we had combined all of our magics and had changed the rules.

The other demons from their realm, the ones that were locked behind barriers, locked away from Malphas, slid their hands through the opening, just to reach their long-lost brother, and pulled Malphas back into the demon realm. He screamed and fought and bled.

But the other demons just smiled and took Malphas

back. His screams were abruptly cut off, his body went limp, and then there was nothing.

Nothing but the quiet that came after death, after the world had changed.

I turned to my mate and threw my arms around him as I cried. He held me as others cheered, wept, and died.

"I've got you," he whispered. "I've got you, always."

I just held him close and let the darkness come over me, for only the moment.

Because I trusted him.

And I knew that this was the ending, but not our ending.

CHAPTER

SEVENTEEN

Steele

As the ashes burned and the world seemed to right itself, it didn't feel real.

It had only been a day since the demon died, or perhaps just been taken back to his realm. A day since we had lost fourteen Pack members and humans who had fought alongside us. In the end, it wasn't just Pack against demon and vampires. No, local humans who had heard the fighting had come out and tried to help. They helped pull the injured to safety, had brought food and water and weapons. They had brought shelter for those who needed it. Witches from a nearby city who were not part of the coven had helped heal who they could. Pack members who had not fought alongside us because they had been protecting their dens, or weren't soldiers, had even come to help.

The government contacted my Alpha, and that was a conversation that I didn't want anything to do with. In the end, they were pleased to hear that the vampire problem might be ending. Because their master was gone, their leaders. There would be cleanup, but I didn't know what else might happen.

In the days since everything had changed, we were healing. Nothing felt real.

"Are you okay?" my mate asked as I pulled on my jeans, still drying from the shower.

I looked at her, at the bruise on her cheek, the bandage on her arm, and I wanted to growl. They had hurt my mate, and I'd almost lost her. How the hell was I supposed to come to terms with that?

She looked towards my glare and shook her head. "I asked if you were okay, but I'm fine. You got hurt far worse than I did. You barely let anybody near me."

"You nearly died," I snarled.

"And you almost died too. But we didn't. We lost friends, but we're here. We survived. And now we have to do everything that we said would come after."

She sat on the bed in her long dress, both of us

knowing that we needed to meet with our friends soon to discuss what happened. We had barely gotten any sleep, the cleanup taking most of the night and into the early morning. But eventually we had crashed, holding onto one another, making love into the morning. We needed to touch each other, to be with each other.

And figuring out who we were felt like a faraway problem that didn't make any sense.

I knelt in front of her, wearing only my jeans, still unbuttoned. I put my hands on her thighs, and she smiled down at me.

"We're going to be late if you're spending some time down there," she teased, but I saw the sadness in her gaze.

She was trying to act as if nothing had happened. But it had.

Sawyer had been hurt, though he would be fine. He was still with the Healers, unconscious, but hopefully waking up soon.

Wynter had been hurt as well, but she was already back to work, following Wren around and healing when she could. She was a nurse, cleaning what didn't need to be seen to by the Healer.

Skye and Chase were both still recovering, but Skye had immediately gone to her parents, taking her daughter, while Chase looked around, watching as we tried to heal as a Pack.

"Everything has changed, even though it doesn't really feel real that the demon is gone."

Jade slid her hands through my hair and studied my face. "Not at all. But we did it. You did it."

That made me laugh, and I shook my head. "You did it, Jade. All of you. You brought us together."

"And you were strong enough to take charge while others faltered, because we all needed each other." She let out a shaky breath and I squeezed her knees before moving so I could cup her cheeks.

"I don't know what I would've done if I'd lost you."

"I don't know either. I was so afraid that that was going to be the end. That we would sacrifice everything for our people, knowing it was the right thing to do, before you and I even had a chance."

I wiped away a tear, my heart breaking for this strong woman who never let herself falter.

"I'm going to say something I should have said before the battle. Before I almost lost you. In fact, I was going to try to say it right before everything changed."

She looked at me then and pressed her lips together.

"I love you, Jade. All of you. Your strength, who we are together. I've known you for over a year now, and I feel like I'm getting to know you more with each passing day. You're my firebird, my flame. And I love you so damn much."

I wasn't good with words, I wasn't good with pouring out my heart. But I didn't really have another choice. I'd almost lost her, and maybe being a little vulnerable was the only way to keep her.

She was so damn strong, and I was afraid if I wasn't careful, I would lose her. Not in battle, but from her strength. And then she slid off the bed and knelt in front of me to cup my face. I smiled at her.

"What is it?"

"I love you too. But why do you look so scared that I'm going to walk away? We're still mates. I made a choice. We both did. And I love you so damn much. I never thought I would have this. But I do. So neither one of us gets to walk away. We just get to go into the future and figure out what the hell we're doing."

My wolf howled, and the hybrid inside me purred, a new feeling.

"So, you're mine?"

"I've always been yours, even if it took me a little while to figure it out."

When I brushed my lips against hers, I sighed, knowing that this was the future I hadn't realized I craved. Hadn't realized I'd wanted.

I kissed her again, and she groaned into me.

I wanted more, we both needed it, but when my alarm went off, I knew we didn't have the time.

"Pack meeting?" she whispered.

"Pack meeting. We all need to be there."

She nodded softly. "Of course. We'll always be there."

I kissed her again, ignoring the alarm for a moment, before we stood up and made our way to Chase's house.

The new Alpha's new house was big enough for us all. I knew this would be the first of many meetings held here. Where we would have to figure out exactly how we would heal as a Pack.

We were the last ones to arrive, which didn't surprise me. We were newly mated and had also been some of the final people to leave the battlefield other than the Alpha couple.

Skye sat in an armchair, her daughter sleeping in her arms. Chase stood behind her, speaking with Cruz. It was odd to think that none of us had known they were brothers for so long. But then again, it had taken a while for us to truly understand that. There had been magic involved hiding it from us. Magic had hid a lot from us. But Blade was gone, his legacy defeated. The demon was gone, and now we would find a way to work with the damage he left behind.

Me.

Audrey and Gavin moved through the house, talking with each other and others as they set out food so we could eat while we talked. As a Beta, it was her job to take care of the Pack in any way she could. To see to our needs, in ways that we might not even realize. So, if we didn't know we were hungry because we were focused on other things, she would make sure we were fed. She kept the Pack cohesive, she and Cruz, the Heir, would ensure anything that slipped through the cracks because we were at war would be handled.

Dara sat next to Wren, their heads close together as they spoke. Wren looked exhausted, and I understood. She had nearly wiped herself out protecting everybody and healing them.

Sawyer wasn't here, and it felt odd because Jade was missing him, but we would find a way to bring him in. To take the next steps to make sure that we never lost him.

Hayes sat in the corner, rubbing his chest, and I knew that he was stressed out because of all the emotions in the room.

There were others here; my lieutenants, elders. People were eating and drinking, trying to heal and come to terms with what had just happened. This was Pack. Something we had almost lost.

I took an empty seat and forced Jade to sit on my lap since there weren't many seats left. She just rolled her eyes, and I held in a laugh at the way the elders smiled at me. They nodded, approving of our mating, and I was glad. Because we needed this security, needed the matings that had come for us over these past few years, after so many years of none.

Chase cleared his throat as we all settled in, and he looked among us, his hand held firmly in Skye's.

"Things have changed, like we all know. We defeated the demon because of all of you." He looked at me proudly, then looked at each person in the room, one by one. "Each and every single one of you sacrificed everything you had. And when we have the Pack circle tonight, to mourn those we lost, we'll continue to live in their legacy. Their sacrifice will not be in vain. The demon is gone, and from all accounts, it's never coming back."

"Good riddance," I growled.

Chase nodded, as everyone else began to agree, murmuring their assent. "There are still vampires out there, something we're going to have to deal with. But the Packs around the world and the governments are all on our side. We'll figure out a way."

"And perhaps there are those good vampires out there, the ones that were in hiding. Maybe we can find them, and they can help," Jade said.

I saw the skepticism in some gazes, but perhaps she was right. Perhaps there were vampires who didn't want to murder us. But I wasn't quite sure if I believed that.

"Our Pack bonds are stronger than ever. But now with the influx of magic, we're changing. All of the dens are.

It's been a long time coming, and we're finding our way. We are going to figure this out. We will mourn our losses and rebuild. And we will never again fall victim to what the demon brought us. Because he's gone, and we are Aspens."

He continued to talk, and I nodded along, but then there was another voice in my head. One I had never thought to hear again.

The moon goddess whispered, and I listened. And when Jade stiffened, I knew she heard her too.

You are of my image as well, my wolf. And for whatever legacy you give, for your future offspring, whatever the demon did will not be passed on. Your children will be safe. The only way to create a hybrid is through biting and runes and the demon's blood. That is my gift to you. The only thing I can do. Any future you desire is yours. I am watching. And I am waiting.

Chase continued to talk, to go over plans about rebuilding and what the Pack circle would entail. He spoke of the other Packs and what was coming and who needed to be here. But I sat there, holding Jade close as the ramifications of the moon goddess's voice hit me.

I was a hybrid. A new paranormal element that we did not understand. But my children wouldn't be burdened with this, and that was something I could never thank the moon goddess enough for.

Later, we would come together as a Pack again, to mourn under the full moon as we ran in our shifter forms, and let our magic infuse us.

We were the Aspens, and we were figuring out who we were.

We had been born into hate and rage. But we had healed once, and we would do it again.

Malphas and the traitors were gone, the demons were defeated.

There were still humans who didn't want us, who were now part of the Human Union who were very vocal in their anti-shifter hate. But they weren't the loudest. They would never be.

There was still the unknown out there, but for now we were enough.

I held my mate in my arms as we made plans for a future I had always been worried we would never have.

We were the Aspens. We had fought and we had prevailed. And we would continue to fight.

No matter what darkness came at us next.

CHAPTER
EIGHTEEN

Jade

A LARGE HAND SLID UP MY SIDE AND MY LIPS twitched into a smile, even though my eyes were still closed. I had no idea what time it was. I could sense the moon's phase, knew that it was the morning, but I had no concept of time beyond that. Only that strong hand on my hip and the bond pulsing between us.

I scooted closer to him, pressing my backside to his groin. He was hard, fully awake, and I just smiled.

When he slid his hand over my thigh and lifted it, I held back a groan. And then he was sliding deep inside me, one hand keeping me steady, the other wrapped around me so he could cup my breast.

I finally opened my eyes and tilted my head so I could see him. It was barely morning, the light just sliding through the curtains.

I could see his face, outlined in shadow. I loved this man. He grinned at me, slowly working his way in and out of me, before he leaned forward and captured my lips. I groaned into him, wanting, needing.

He was everything, and it was hard for me to remember just to breathe, to move with him.

Because none of this felt real.

I was the firebird, he was mine. We were each other's in every way, and yet part of me had never thought we could ever have this moment. He was agony and ecstasy and so tangled up in my soul that I knew that we were one, two separate entities who were part of each other forever.

And that wasn't the promise I had made to myself all those years ago, when I had been forced to try to learn who I could be on my own.

He kissed me with abandon, and I smiled into him, kissing him back, moving with him.

And when he slid out of me, I reached for him, my mate, my Steele. My strength. But he wasn't gone for long.

Because then I was on my back and he was between my legs, and I was arching into him.

He slid his hands down my thighs once again and lifted me up as he sank into me. I stretched around him.

"The best way to wake up," I whispered into him.

He smiled at me, his wolf in his eyes, and I slid my hands up his chest, over his shoulders, to cup his face.

"I love you," he whispered.

It was gruff, a little rough, and all him.

My Enforcer, my mate. We didn't do emotions, we did sarcasm and hate. We threw things at each other, and we laughed and then we made love.

We weren't maudlin or so rosy that we couldn't see past the end of our nose. But we were everything. We were starting. We were beginning.

And in this moment we could be warm, we could be exactly who we needed to be with one another.

I smiled at him and let the fire burn within my gaze. "I love you too, my mate."

He winked at me before he moved again, a little harder, a little rougher. I slid my hands down his back, my fingernails digging into his skin. He groaned before he leaned forward and nipped at the place where he had marked me as his. He didn't need to do it again, didn't need to mark me for everyone to know. All shifters and magical beings would know I was his.

Hell, with the way he continued to claim me in public, far more territorial than I ever thought possible, even humans without the sense of magic would be able to see that I was claimed by an Enforcer.

I had been marked by him, and as I grinned, he was marked in flames as well.

Fire danced along my fingertips as I played along his back.

"Branding me, are you?" he asked as he leisurely made love to me, and both of us sucked in deep breaths.

"Always."

And then he picked up the pace, and before I could think, we were rolling, and I was hovering over him, riding him to completion.

My body clenched, my nipples tightening, and then I was coming, the fire within me burning to embers.

I had long ago fallen for my mate, and I hadn't even realized it.

And in this moment, we were one. He came, filling me, both of us groaning and reaching for one another.

This was just the beginning, just a way to wake up, a way to greet our morning.

And I had never been more blessed than I was in this moment.

I collapsed on top of him, sweaty, exhausted, and yet wired.

"You're so damn beautiful," he whispered, running his hands over my hair.

"You're just saying that because your cock is still inside me."

I clenched my inner muscles, and he let out a groan that did things to me.

"You're a vixen. A temptress."

"I'm a witch, thank you very much."

I pressed another kiss to his lips, and he grinned.

"Are you ready for today?"

"I'm not sure. I'm a little nervous."

He cupped my face and shook his head. "You don't have to be nervous. You're better at speeches and being in front of people than I am. I just order them around."

"You don't think I order people around enough?" I teased.

"I think that you could do whatever you want. If you'd like to order me around, I'll let you."

I snorted and leaned down, kissing his lips. "You only say that because we're alone."

"That is true."

I sighed into him, and then my alarm went off, and we laughed before we rolled off the bed and got ready for our day.

We had cleanup and healing to do. Our Pack was safe, our coven was safe.

And we were still learning who we needed to be as a power. But the enemy was gone, turned to dust and ash. And we were still here, victorious.

I was still learning the ropes of what it meant to be a Pack member, a coven leader, a mate. What it meant to live in a world where they knew who I was, what my power could do. That there was no longer a demon waiting for me to fall.

There was no longer true evil beckoning us into death and temptation.

I was bent over, wearing a towel and trying to pick what I was going to wear for the day, when the door to the bedroom slammed open, and Dara and Cruz stood there, grinning at us.

"What the hell?" Steele growled, pulling on his jeans on the rest of the way.

Dara kept her gaze averted and was only looking at me, thankfully.

"Today is a very big day, and that means you get to come with me while I get you ready, and you don't get to see your mate until the ceremony."

"I know what today is," I said as I laughed, standing there in my towel with my hands on my hips. They had already seen me naked before, when I had been nearly burned to a crisp, so I didn't really care in this moment. And while nudity didn't tend to matter to shifters, I was newly mated to a wolf in the room, and I knew that he wasn't pleased that Cruz could see so much of me.

"Come on now, I'll take care of you, big boy," Cruz said with a joking sneer, as Steele flipped him off.

"Eyes off my mate."

"Don't worry, he only has eyes for me," Dara said with a laugh, and then Steele looked at me, wolf in his gaze.

"Under the moonlight?"

"If not before."

Cruz sighed and shook his head. "You've fallen so quickly."

"Damn straight he has, just like you have," Dara called out. Cruz blew her a kiss and Dara caught it, holding it to her chest.

I just rolled my eyes. "You're a death witch. Start acting like a death witch."

"And you're a firebird from hell. You should start acting like one too. Oh, wait, too late."

I flipped her off and we both laughed, before she nearly tackled me in her hug.

"You're going to have a wonderful evening tonight and the ceremony is going to be beautiful, and the Pack will be there, the coven will be there, the rest of the alliance will be there. It's going to be amazing."

"Why are you talking so quickly? Is everything okay?"

I looked at her then, at the way she carried herself, and blinked.

"You're pregnant."

Dara put her finger over her lips and winked. And as tears formed, I threw my arms around her and hugged her tight.

This was the beginning, a new chance.

Because I never thought this moment would ever come. I knew Dara had thought this moment would never come.

She was bringing a new life into the world, a world filled with choice, and perhaps danger, but with hope.

Later that night, when I stood in front of the Packs, wearing a long flowy red dress, and held hands with my mate, I knew that this was our moment.

"As Alpha, it is my duty and my joy to watch you as mates. To declare you as mates. And to share with the world your bond of truth, determination, and fiery steel," he said with a wink.

Everyone laughed at the horrible pun, but my mate just grinned at me.

"He's been waiting a very long time to say that," he said, deadpan.

"It's okay, I'm sure I'll make a lot of Steele jokes by the end of the evening."

Everybody tittered, some outright laughing, as Steele

just rolled his eyes and kissed me again.

We stood under the moon as the goddess herself blessed us, and I knew that this was our time.

Our moment.

We were all changing, but settling into who we could be. Who we had to be.

Audrey and Gavin stood to one side, hands clasped, and smiled wide. They had mated under darkness and had come out stronger. They had shown me who I could be if I just believed.

Chase stood by us, but his mate Skye sat with the others, their child in her arms. The future of this Pack.

Nico, Cole, and Adalyn sat with the others as well, no longer Aspen Pack or Redwood Pack members, but the Alphas of the Centrals. They came with their Pack, as did the Redwoods. Dara and Cruz stood with us, while our other friends sat in the crowd, blessing this union, our mating.

Sawyer stood by me as well, as my friend from my past, someone who would always be part of my future. He had nearly died for me, had nearly died for our people and the Aspens would never forget that. I would never forget that.

I knew that we were never going to be truly healed. That we would always remain marked and scarred.

The fact that Novah was there at all, sitting by Wren

and the others, hollow-eyed but determined, reminded me that we had not all come out of this unscathed. We had lost part of ourselves in this war. We had lost the trust that had come with who we were.

I didn't know how she would come through this, nor how the others who had lost so much would fare. But I knew we would. Because we wouldn't be alone.

And as we were once again declared mates, and my mate kissed me, I held on to Steele, and our future.

The demon was gone, our Pack was safe. And our alliance would be able to flourish. The coven was once again whole, and magic was starting to flourish. And not only that, but witches who had been hiding for generations were starting to come to us, knowing they could be safe.

We had done that. Somehow, we had made that happen.

It wasn't our ending, it was only a beginning.

We had changed. And we would change.

But finally, we Aspens were free. And we were safe.

As my mate held me, and others laughed around us, I knew that Steele and I would do all in our power to keep that so.

Because we had vowed to each other, and to our Pack.

Long live the Aspens. And long live the power we held together.

CHAPTER
NINETEEN

Sawyer

MY HEAD ACHED, AND I HOPED IT WAS ALLERGIES though I knew it wasn't.

Bruises covered my side, but they were healing. They shouldn't have been healing this quickly though. No, I was just tired, not thinking straight.

I staggered through the room, knowing I needed something, I just didn't know what it was.

My ribs ached, as did my hips, everything from when I had hit the ground with such velocity that I thought I had broken everything in my body.

I hadn't though, but I could still feel the pain.

I wasn't as strong as those who fought around me. No, they all could take a hit and keep going. They were stabbed and clawed and bitten and could keep fighting.

I had stood by a wolf who had been shot in the arm and kept going, despite the pain I had seen in their eyes.

They had felt that pain. Having the ability to shift into a wolf or a bear or a cat didn't negate the fact that they felt pain.

Though the Healer had been able to help me because I was Pack and we could use Pack bonds, I wasn't a shifter.

I wasn't a magic user. I didn't have Jade's power, or Dara's. Although I wasn't sure I wanted their kind of power.

It seemed odd to me that this was my life now, contemplating the power that different paranormal creatures had.

I was born human and had lived as human until recently.

And then I had stood on a precipice and made a choice. To follow my friend into darkness.

Because it wasn't as if there was light behind me.

I ran my hands over my face as somebody knocked on the door, and I quickly yanked a shirt over my head and tried not to stagger towards the fist on the door.

"You okay?" Hayes asked, and I looked up, my head

tilting back at a severe angle to see the big man who stood in front of me.

He was the only polar bear I knew. In fact, before joining this Pack, I hadn't even realized that bear and cat shifters existed. But there were a few cats, including a lynx and a golden panther. There were others now, though they were pretty secretive of what they were. And as I had my own reasons to keep who I was and my past private, I understood it.

But Hayes was the only polar bear in existence for all I knew.

Though he had dark-brown hair and a big bushy beard, his eyes were that light blue that screamed supernatural.

He was tall, wide, and looked like he could throw you against a wall and you wouldn't even notice that big paw coming at you.

He was also the Omega of the Pack and could feel every emotion the entire Pack felt, including mine.

I quickly tamped down on that bond, just how Hayes had taught me when I'd first been blooded into the Pack and he had shown me how to keep my emotions my own.

He raised a brow at me and stormed his way in.

But he wasn't alone.

Of course he wasn't alone.

She walked in, her light-blond hair tucked behind her ears, her bright green eyes intense.

This small woman, a lynx, smiled up at me, but didn't meet my gaze.

She was a submissive shifter, but she held a level of power that others didn't.

Wren was the Healer of the Aspen Pack.

She was the one who saved us all.

She had saved my life, and I didn't want to resent her for it.

Because it was her duty, but I hated that I was weak enough to not be able to save myself.

"I'm here to check on your wounds, and I guess Hayes is too," she said with a wry smile.

She might be quieter than everyone else in this Pack, less growly, and couldn't meet my gaze every time, but she was feisty.

I liked that.

"I'm fine. Bruises are healing, and I'm just about to jump in the shower."

Not quite a lie, not quite the truth.

"You sure tamped down on your emotions as soon as you saw me," Hayes said as he sank into my armchair.

I lived on the Pack lands now, as my house had been burned down when Jade's had a while ago. I was still finding furniture that I liked, and I was borrowing what I needed until I found it. I had a decent enough savings account, and I still had a job. But I wasn't great at actually buying things to fit my needs.

"Come on, take off that shirt, let me see your bruises."

I raised a brow, I couldn't help it.

"Really. In front of Hayes?"

Hayes barked out a laugh and just shook his head.

"I'm pretty sure that Wren could take you down with her tiny little pinky. She doesn't need me to help you undress."

Wren scowled between us.

"Are you sure you want to go there, Hayes? When I know where your eye is?"

That shut the Omega up quickly, and I looked between them, eyes wide.

"I always thought, well," I cleared my throat. "I always thought the two of you..."

Wren finally met my gaze before she burst out laughing.

"No. Not even a little. We're like siblings."

"Siblings who fight," Hayes growled.

"No, he has his eye on someone else, or should I say someones?"

Hayes flipped her off, and I had never seen the big man do anything untoward towards Wren. It was shocking, and it just made me laugh, despite the panic settling inside me as a new wave of something I didn't want to name hit me.

Hayes leaned forward, eyes narrowed, and I knew he had felt it.

When Wren looked between us, she frowned.

"What is it?" she asked.

"I'm just tired. I'm human, you know, it takes me longer to recover."

"Maybe, but you'll let me know if things feel off? I worry."

I lifted my shirt so she could see the bruises. "You don't need to worry about me. You do a good job. All of you do. I'm damn lucky to have you guys in my corner."

Wren looked at me then, and there was something in her eyes I couldn't quite name.

I wanted to reach out, tuck that hair right back behind her ears since it had fallen. But I didn't.

Wren didn't want me. She was older than me by a few decades, which, in the supernatural world, didn't matter. But in the human world, it meant that my life would be cut short, and she would keep living, and would one day find her mate.

I was attracted to her, and when she met my gaze, I realized that maybe I just needed a damn nap.

When I looked over at Hayes and saw the pity in his

gaze, I knew that I hadn't quite tamped down on those emotions well enough.

I cleared my throat and took a step back. "Thanks for checking on me. I am going to shower. And maybe take a walk. Then sleep. I promise I'm taking care of myself."

"You better," Wren said, as she passed her hands over the bruises.

I swallowed hard, ignoring the touch. Or at least trying to.

Hayes cleared his throat and stood up.

No, I hadn't hidden that emotion quite well at all.

"Come on, Wren. He's fine."

"I like the look of them. They're healing quickly. That's good. I don't work on humans that often. Only really Wynter these days."

Hayes narrowed his gaze at Wren as she smiled at him. Oh. So that's where the big bear was looking. I had to wonder who else he was looking at. But that wasn't my place. Not when I was still figuring out what the hell was going on with me.

Nothing. Nothing was going on with me. And if I kept telling myself that, it would make sense.

Finally, the two left, but not after giving me one last look. Hayes with a look that said he wanted answers, but neither one of us were willing to speak. And there was something in Wren's gaze again, but I didn't know what it was.

But I knew I couldn't answer whatever question was there.

I closed the door, locking it behind them. Not that a locked door would keep out a shifter if they needed to get in.

I made sure the blinds were closed, before all my energy left me and I nearly fell, making my way to the mirror.

My hands on either side of it, I stared, and I was so afraid of what I was going to see.

Because Wren hadn't fixed everything.

She wouldn't be able to.

It didn't make any sense that I could still think, that I could still breathe. But here I was, changing the rules.

And as I lifted my lip, I let out a curse.

The fangs that had arrived soon after the fight glimmered in the light, and I closed my mouth, knowing I'd have to tell them soon. Knowing I'd have to end it all or find the group the elder had said existed.

But as a wave of hunger slid over me, a hunger that wasn't for food, I cursed.

This might just be my own ending.

***

IF YOU'RE IN THE MOOD FOR A PARANORMAL romance outside the world of the Aspens, try The Ravenwood Coven with Dawn Unearthed

WANT TO READ A SPECIAL **BONUS EPILOGUE** FEATURING JADE AND STEELE? **CLICK HERE!**

A NOTE FROM CARRIE ANN

Thank you so much for reading **Marked in Flames!**

Years ago, when I first thought of the Aspen Pack series, I knew things would change within the world. I wanted to see what would happen when a demon came back and if we introduced a new kind of supernatural element: the vampire in my shifter world.

Jade and Steele were dynamic from the start and I'm so glad they are the ones closing out the series...for now.

Is this the end of the Aspen Pack series?

Right now it is...but you see...there are a few more characters that need HEAs...I'm just not ready for them yet.

So thank you for being part of this journey. And as always, long live the Pack!

The Aspen Pack Series:

Book 1: Etched in Honor

Book 2: Hunted in Darkness

Book 3: Mated in Chaos

Book 4: Harbored in Silence

Book 5: Marked in Flames

And if you're in the mood for a paranormal romance outside the world of the Aspens:

The Ravenwood Coven Series:

Book 1: Dawn Unearthed

Book 2: Dusk Unveiled

Book 3: Evernight Unleashed

WANT TO READ A SPECIAL BONUS EPILOGUE FEATURING JADE AND STEELE? CLICK HERE!

If you want to make sure you know what's coming next from me, you can sign up for my newsletter at www. CarrieAnnRyan.com; follow me on twitter at @CarrieAnnRyan, or like my Facebook page. I also have a Facebook Fan Club where we have trivia, chats, and other goodies. You guys are the reason I get to do what I do and I thank you.

Make sure you're signed up for my MAILING LIST so you can know when the next releases are available as well as find giveaways and FREE READS.

Happy Reading!

ALSO FROM CARRIE ANN RYAN

The Montgomery Ink Legacy Series:

Book 1: Bittersweet Promises

Book 2: At First Meet

Book 2.5: Happily Ever Never

Book 3: Longtime Crush

Book 4: Best Friend Temptation

Book 5: Last First Kiss

Book 6: His Second Chance

The Wilder Brothers Series:

Book 1: One Way Back to Me

Book 2: Always the One for Me

Book 3: The Path to You

Book 4: Coming Home for Us

Book 5: Stay Here With Me

Book 6: Finding the Road to Us

Book 7: Moments for You

Book 8: A Wilder Wedding

The First Time Series:

Book 1: Good Time Boyfriend

Book 2: Last Minute Fiancé

The Aspen Pack Series:

Book 1: Etched in Honor

Book 2: Hunted in Darkness

Book 3: Mated in Chaos

Book 4: Harbored in Silence

Book 5: Marked in Flames

The Montgomery Ink: Fort Collins Series:

Book 1: Inked Persuasion

Book 2: Inked Obsession

Book 3: Inked Devotion

Book 3.5: Nothing But Ink

Book 4: Inked Craving

Book 5: Inked Temptation

The Montgomery Ink: Boulder Series:

Book 1: Wrapped in Ink

Book 2: Sated in Ink

Book 3: Embraced in Ink

The On My Own Series:

The Promise Me Series:

The Ravenwood Coven Series:

Book 1: Dawn Unearthed

Book 2: Dusk Unveiled

Book 3: Evernight Unleashed

The Talon Pack:

Book 1: Tattered Loyalties

Book 2: An Alpha's Choice

Book 3: Mated in Mist

Book 4: Wolf Betrayed

Book 5: Fractured Silence

Book 6: Destiny Disgraced

Book 7: Eternal Mourning

Book 8: Strength Enduring

Book 9: Forever Broken

Book 10: Mated in Darkness

Book 11: Fated in Winter

Redwood Pack Series:

Book 1: An Alpha's Path

Book 2: A Taste for a Mate

Book 3: Trinity Bound

Book 3.5: A Night Away

Book 5: <u>Fierce Enchantment</u>

Book 6: <u>An Immortal's Song</u>

Book 7: <u>Prowled Darkness</u>

Book 8: Dante's Circle Reborn

Holiday, Montana Series:

Book 1: <u>Charmed Spirits</u>

Book 2: <u>Santa's Executive</u>

Book 3: <u>Finding Abigail</u>

Book 4: <u>Her Lucky Love</u>

Book 5: Dreams of Ivory

The Branded Pack Series:

(Written with Alexandra Ivy)

Book 1: <u>Stolen and Forgiven</u>

Book 2: <u>Abandoned and Unseen</u>

Book 3: <u>Buried and Shadowed</u>

ABOUT THE AUTHOR

Carrie Ann Ryan is the New York Times and USA Today bestselling author of contemporary, paranormal, and young adult romance. Her works include the Montgomery Ink, Redwood Pack, Fractured Connections, and Elements of Five series, which have sold over 3.0 million books worldwide. She started writing while in graduate school for her advanced degree in chemistry and hasn't stopped since. Carrie Ann has written over seventy-five novels and novellas with more in the works. When she's not losing herself in her emotional and action-packed worlds, she's reading as much as she can while wrangling her clowder of cats who have more followers than she does.

www.CarrieAnnRyan.com